Empty Words

Empty Words

Mario Levrero

Translated by Annie McDermott

Minneapolis
2019

Book design by Rachel Holscher

First published in 1996 as *El discurso vacío* by Ediciones Trilce.
Translation rights arranged by Agencia Literaria CBQ SL,
info@agencialiterariacbq.com.

Coffee House Press books are available to the trade through our primary distributor, Consortium Book Sales & Distribution, cbsd.com or (800) 283-3572. For personal orders, catalogs, or other information, write to info@coffeehousepress.org.

Coffee House Press is a nonprofit literary publishing house. Support from private foundations, corporate giving programs, government programs, and generous individuals helps make the publication of our books possible. We gratefully acknowledge their support in detail in the back of this book.

LIBRARY OF CONGRESS CATALOGING-IN-PUBLICATION DATA

Names: Levrero, Mario, author. | McDermott, Annie, translator.
Title: Empty words / Mario Levrero ; translated by Annie McDermott.
Other titles: Discurso vacío. English
Description: First English-language edition. | [Minneapolis, Minnesota] : Coffee House Press, 2019. | "First published in 1996 as El discurso vacío by Ediciones Trilce."
Identifiers: LCCN 2018040460 (print) | LCCN 2018051264 (ebook) | ISBN 9781566895545 (ebook) | ISBN 9781566895460 (trade paperback)
Subjects: LCSH: Authors—Fiction.
Classification: LCC PQ8520.22.E9 (ebook) | LCC PQ8520.22.E9 D513 2019 (print) | DDC 863/.64—dc23
LC record available at https://lccn.loc.gov/2018040460

PRINTED IN THE UNITED STATES OF AMERICA

26 25 24 23 22 21 20 19   1 2 3 4 5 6 7 8

This book and its contents exist in relation to my wife, Alicia, and her world. Although it goes without saying, I should emphasize that this novel is dedicated to Alicia, Juan Ignacio, and Pongo the dog—in other words, to my family.

M. L., MONTEVIDEO, OCTOBER 1996

Contents

Translator's Note

When asked by one interviewer to name his influences, Mario Levrero listed Mandrake the Magician, a comic-strip hero who hypnotized his enemies, along with Lewis Carroll, tango music from the 1940s, detective novels, the Beatles, and the early days of *Tía Vicenta,* a satirical Argentinian current affairs magazine. "It's a mistake to expect literature to come only from literary sources," he said, "like expecting a cheesemaker to eat nothing but cheese." The Levrero archive in Uruguay's University of the Republic is similarly heterogeneous, containing records of homeopathic treatment, a guide to yoga exercises, graphs showing how much time he spent on the computer each day, drawings of the students in his creative writing workshops, and a personal set of homemade tarot cards.

In Latin America, it's said that Chile produces poets, Argentina produces short story writers, Mexico produces novelists, and Uruguay produces "los raros"—the strange ones. Levrero was a raro of the highest order, though he rejected the label, complaining that it meant journalists and critics were forever wanting him to do new strange things. "It would be far more interesting for them if, instead of writing, I committed a murder," he grumbled in a famous "imaginary interview" he conducted with himself. Still, it's hard to think of a more fitting category for this uncategorizable writer who refused to be bound by rules or conventions and for whom the "only thing that matters in literature is writing with as much freedom as you possibly can."

Levrero made his first departure from the conventions of ordinary life at the age of fourteen, when a heart murmur (combined, perhaps, with a dislike of going to lessons) obliged him to stay home from school and spend his days in bed, reading and listening to the tango station Radio Clarín—which, thanks to a system he'd devised involving pieces of string, he could turn on and off without having to get up. He didn't finish high school and has said that the Guardia Nueva tango club in Montevideo served as his university. It was there, for example, that he first heard about James Joyce, and it also gave him the name for the Guardia Nueva secondhand bookshop he ran with a friend throughout his twenties. Though staunchly apolitical in later life, Levrero was briefly a member of the youth wing of the Uruguayan Communist Party and was one of the protesters who ended up with diarrhea after fascists poisoned some chorizo donated to a march in support of Cuba in 1962. (José Mujica, later the president of Uruguay, was on the same march).[1]

In 1966, at the age of twenty-six, Levrero wrote his first novel, *La ciudad (The City).* It was inspired by the work of Kafka: until reading him, Levrero said, he "didn't realize it was possible to tell the truth," and *La ciudad* was "almost an attempt to translate Kafka into Uruguayan." From this point on, Levrero wrote some twenty books, among them the

1 Much of the information in this paragraph is taken from Jesús Montoya Juárez's excellent book *Mario Levrero para armar: Jorge Varlotta y el libertinaje imaginativo* (Ediciones Trilce, 2013).

dreamlike "involuntary trilogy" of *La ciudad, París (Paris),* and *El lugar (The Place);* the rollicking detective-novel parody *Nick Carter se divierte mientras el lector es asesinado y yo agonizo (Nick Carter Enjoys Himself While the Reader Is Murdered and I Expire),* and the autobiographical *El discurso vacío (Empty Words)* and *La novela luminosa* (*The Luminous Novel,* forthcoming from Coffee House Press and And Other Stories)—this last, a book with a 450-page prologue explaining why it was impossible to write the book itself, being widely recognized as his masterpiece. It is astonishing, considering the wildly varied nature of his literary output, that it should all form a coherent whole, and yet it does: everything Levrero wrote is instantly recognizable as his.

The novel *Empty Words,* first published in 1996, is a perfect introduction to the levreriano, or Levrero-esque. It charts the author's attempts to turn his life around using "graphological self-therapy": if he can improve his handwriting, he thinks, he'll be able to improve his personality, "transforming a whole plethora of bad behaviors into good ones and catapulting [himself] blissfully into a life of happiness, joy, money, and success." And yet as he persists with his daily handwriting practice, he comes to realize that the exercises "are becoming less calligraphical and more literary as time goes on." Another kind of text is trying to break through: "a flow, a rhythm, a seemingly empty form" is guiding his hand, and he finds himself continuing to write without knowing what it is that he's writing, hoping to uncover the mystery of this "empty" text as he goes.

This is pure Levrero: for him, writing is both a mystery to be solved and a means of solving it, at once a tool for exploring the unconscious and a by-product of those explorations. Also typically levreriano is the way his efforts to understand this mysterious force are discussed in the same breath as his attempts to give up smoking, complaints about the weather, accounts of his dreams, investigations into the inner workings of his computer, and musings about the behavior of his dog. Levrero writes about all these things in the same unmistakable voice, combining an earnestly matter-of-fact desire to make himself clear with a sardonic, deadpan, and fantastically absurd sense of humor. Here he is on his worsening mental state: "I can feel myself getting more anxious by the day, at a rate I can even represent graphically by means of a curve showing my daily intake of cigarettes." On (short-lived) improvements to his daily routine: "Allow me to record, so it's known in the centuries to come, that I'm writing this at eight thirty in the morning." On trying to program the computer to make sounds: "After a while, I managed to bring about some interesting bird-like cheeping." And practicing writing the letter r, which he finds particularly troublesome: "rhododendron, rower, sombrero, bra-strap, parricide, reverberate, procrastinate, corduroys (I repeat: corduroys)."

Throughout his literary career, Levrero resolutely denied that he had any such thing. He shied away from publicity, rarely left his house or even answered his doorbell toward the end of his life, and used to boast that he was impossible to interview because his voice didn't show up on audio recordings—which he made sure of by speaking in an indecipherable murmur as soon as anyone switched on a tape recorder in his vicinity. And yet, despite his best efforts, he became something of a cult figure in Uruguay and Argentina during his lifetime. Enthusiastic readers and friends went to great lengths to get his work published, and his legendary literary workshops, which focused on liberating the imagination, produced hundreds of students who consider themselves his disciples. Ever since the publication of *La novela luminosa* in 2005, one year after his death, he has been heralded as one of the great Latin American writers of the twentieth century, and it's been an honor and a joy to translate him.

ANNIE MCDERMOTT
LONDON, SEPTEMBER 2018

The Text

Empty Words is a novel formed from two different strands, or groups of texts. One, entitled "Exercises," is a series of short handwriting exercises, written with no other purpose than that. The other, entitled "The Empty Discourse," is a single, unified text that's more "literary" in intention.

The novel in its current form was constructed as a diary. To the "Exercises," which were ordered chronologically, I added the parts of "The Empty Discourse" that correspond to each date, using headings to separate the two. This solution was suggested by Eduardo Abel Giménez as an alternative to my previous method, which had been based on some fairly unreliable typographical variations.

Later, while editing, I removed a few passages and even entire "Exercises," at points to protect my own privacy or other people's, but always with the aim of making the text less boring to read. I also added the odd phrase or paragraph here and there to clarify the meaning of some references. Apart from these minor surgical procedures, this text is faithful to the originals.

M. L., COLONIA, MAY 1993

Empty Words

Prologue

December 22, 1989

Something within me, which is not me, which I search for
Something within me, which I sometimes think is me, but
  never find
Something that shows up for no reason, shines for an instant,
  and then
    vanishes for years
    and years.
Something I also forget.
Something
which is close to love but not quite love,
which could be confused with freedom,
with truth,
with the being's absolute identity—
but which can't be contained in words,
considered in concepts,
or even recorded just as it is.
It is what it is, and it's not mine, and sometimes it's inside me
(but not very often), and when it is,
it remembers itself,
I remember it, I think it and know it.

It's not worth searching; the more you look
the more distant it seems, the better it hides.
You have to forget it completely,
almost to the point of suicide
(because without it life is worthless)
(because those who've never known it think life is worthless)
(which is why the world creaks as it turns).

This is my illness, my reason for living.

* * *

I've seen God
flash by in the eyes of a whore,
give me signs with an ant's antennae,
turn to wine in a bunch of grapes in the dust,
appear before me in a dream as a disgusting giant slug;
I've seen God in a sunbeam, giving slanted life to the
afternoon,
in my lover's purple jacket after a storm,
in a red traffic light,
in a stubborn bee sucking at a slight, wilted flower,
trampled and sad in the Plaza Congreso.
I have even seen God in a church.

March 11, 1990

I dreamed I was a photographer, running to and fro enthusiastically with a camera. I was somewhere very large, a kind of warehouse or depot, though it could also have been the lobby of a big hotel, and I was trying to find the right angle from which to photograph two lesbians so that, although they were located fairly far apart in the huge space and even at different heights (maybe one was up some stairs), their mouths met in a way that suggested a kiss. They both had their lips painted a deep red. The one closest to the camera was in profile; the other, who was higher up, was facing me.

Later I find myself aboard an enormous double-decker bus—on the roof, or in an open-top area on the upper level. I'm photographing or filming scenes from a big city. All of a sudden there's a commotion, something happening in the distance, like waves crashing over skyscrapers. People tell me it's the end of the world. I photograph the chaos, which is far away and difficult to make out, and feel excited and strangely elated. I wake up with tachycardia.

When I go back to sleep, someone's telling a story (and I see the story taking place), or I'm watching a film, although somehow I'm also part of the action. There's a brown rabbit buried in the snow, and he's burrowing to and fro under the surface, moving quickly from place to place. I start to worry he's going to hit something, a tree or a rock, because suddenly he seems hesitant, but then I find that he's learned to communicate with a dove by means of a system that, in the dream, was explained in great detail. The dove was flying above the rabbit's head, above the snow, and guiding his movements.

Part One: Exercises

September 10, 1990

My graphological self-therapy begins today. This method (suggested a while ago by a crazy friend) stems from the notion—which is central to graphology—that there's a profound connection between a person's handwriting and his or her character, and from the behaviorist tenet that changes in behavior can lead to changes on a psychological level. The idea, then, is that by changing the behavior observed in a person's handwriting, it may be possible to change other things about that person.

My aims at this stage of the therapeutic endeavor are fairly modest. At first, I'm going to practice writing by hand. I won't be attempting calligraphy, but I'll at least try to manage a script that anyone could read—myself included, because these days my writing's often so bad that not even I can decipher it.

Another of my immediate aims is to develop large, expansive handwriting in contrast to my microscopic scrawl of recent years. A further, more ambitious aim is to make my writing more <u>uniform</u>, since at the moment I mix cursive script and printed letters quite arbitrarily. I'll try to remember how each letter is written by hand, more or less the way I learned in school. The idea is to achieve a kind of continuous writing, "without lifting the pen" in the middle of words. I think this will help me improve my concentration and the continuity of my thoughts, which are currently all over the place.

September 11

Day two of handwriting therapy. I was pleasantly surprised yesterday when I gave the page I'd written to Alicia and she found it easy to read. Now I'm trying to do three things: (1) keep the letters to a suitable size, (2) get back to real handwriting, without printed letters creeping in all the time, and (3) not lift my pen—that is, only dotting the i's and crossing the t's once I've finished writing the whole word. This last point might be the most difficult, though the "real" handwriting isn't exactly a walk in the park.

At first, looking at what I've written so far and comparing it to what I wrote yesterday, there seems to be some progress. Today's writing, however—though larger and more legible—reveals a certain nervousness; I'm writing more quickly now than I was yesterday. But I also notice that the letters are more "separate," more spaced-out within each word, less bunched together than before. As if each one had recovered its individuality. All in all, I'm happy with today's work and the improvements from yesterday. I know I'm still a long way from achieving my goals, even the most basic ones; I know I still can't remember how to write some capital letters and some lowercase ones. But everything will come with time.

September 24

I'm returning to my handwriting therapy after an extended interruption, since my mother's stroke took me away from home. During that time I really missed this daily discipline: though I haven't been doing these exercises long, they've already started to seem like an entirely positive—and enjoyable—habit, and a big help when it comes to centering my inner self and preparing for a more orderly, purposeful, and balanced day ahead.

Now there's an interruption from the outside world, in the form of a small, flustered woman calling to me in an angry voice, revealing unmistakable signs of impatience. However, I try not to lose the slow, deliberate, meditative rhythm of my writing, because I know these daily exercises will do wonders for my health and character, transforming a whole plethora of bad behaviors into good ones and catapulting me blissfully into a life of happiness, joy, money, and success with women and in other games of chance. And now, without further ado, I bid myself farewell until the same time tomorrow, or earlier if possible.

September 25

My handwriting therapy continues. Yesterday, the person who usually reviews these pages said the writing had become a bit more difficult to read after the long break. I think there are at least two reasons for this, and one, of course, is lack of practice. The other, which is interesting to consider, is the fact that yesterday, unlike previously, the act of saying something and the question of how to say it (in other words, literature) felt more important than the pure calligraphical exercise.

Right. I'm getting distracted again and paying too little attention to the handwriting and too much to the subject matter, which is anti-therapeutic, at least in the therapeutic context I've chosen. I'm sure this shift in focus would be welcome and constructive in other therapeutic contexts, but I can't go mixing the different elements here. I need to stick to what I set out to do: producing a kind of insubstantial but legible text.

I think my handwriting's clearer today than yesterday. Let's see what the person who usually reviews these pages has to say about it.

September 26

More handwriting practice today. It's clear from the first strokes of my pen that I'm feeling down, that my heart's not in it, and I have no interest in talking myself around. Maybe I'm coming down with a cold, caught from Juan Ignacio or Pongo the dog, who's feeling down today too. There could also be something about the weather that's bothering us all. Most likely, though, is that my mood is the result of a dream I had this morning involving piles of dead, rotting, blood-covered rats and my grandmother. The dream, in turn, must be the result of everything I've been through in recent days (between the twelfth and twenty-first of this month). The figure of my grandmother in the dream surely corresponds to that of my mother in real life, since when I was at my mother's side during those days, I often found myself thinking about her and my grandmother, and about how much my mother has come to resemble her mother with age. What's more, there were very few moments during that period when I had a clear sense of being next to my mother: instead I felt, with a profound, spontaneous certainty that came from deep within me, that she was my grandmother.

In my dream last night, my grandmother lived in a house I was staying in; I was just passing through, as if visiting a new place, maybe a seaside resort. There were piles of dead rats in my bedroom, and then I started seeing them elsewhere around the house as well, especially in the kitchen. I said something about "calling the council or the police," but in the end I didn't. It was late, and besides, my grandmother seemed perfectly fine with what was going on, treating this situation that to me seemed so out of the ordinary as if it were the most normal thing in the world.

September 27

The important thing is to be very patient and concentrate hard, trying as much as possible to draw the letters one by one and giving no thought to the meanings of the words they're forming—an operation which is almost the complete opposite of literature (especially because it involves slowing down my thinking, which is used to my typewriter and always wants to jump ahead, suggest new ideas, and make new connections between thoughts and images, concerned—it's part of the job, I suppose—with the continuity and coherence of what's being said).

I need to stick to simple phrases, then, however empty or insubstantial they sound. The moment I start paying attention to the content, I lose sight of the point of this therapy (i.e., drawing every single letter).

As I write this, Juan Ignacio is being a nuisance and trying to get his mother's attention, while she's enjoying a rare moment of relaxation and watching a film I recommended on the VCR. I notice Ignacio has been brought up not to accept his mother's relaxing, having fun, or even being ill; when she does any of these things, he gets more demanding than usual, complaining and sulking intolerably. There's an unhealthy equilibrium in this household and how it functions, the product of a set of habits or patterns of behavior that don't do anyone any good. These patterns have been adopted gradually through "chance and necessity," and the idea of altering even one of them leads to unease, nervousness, or even a crisis in any of the original members of the family unit.

September 28

I ought to get ahold of some phrases for practicing letters with "stems," the sort of thing I used when I was learning to type. "European port," "I'd like a table," "quite a squint," "tomato ketchup," "fool's gold." But monotonous activities like that are so tedious. I'd rather make slower progress—a few steps forward, a few steps back—and often let my writing get smaller or more misshapen as my hand races wildly across the page in pursuit of my thoughts. Because I can't stand repetitive, routine tasks, and—in writing, if not in life—want my experiences to be somehow new, unexpected, adventurous. Like, for example, my investigations into a computer whose instruction manual is incomplete.

Earlier this week, after hours and days of hard work and research, and various (literally) thunderous failures, I persuaded the computer to make a noise. Then I managed to do it more consistently, <u>knowing</u> what I was doing, and yesterday I was finally able to make <u>music</u> (a basic, rudimentary little tune, but music nonetheless), all without the manual so much as mentioning the word "sound." I managed it thanks to a program in BASIC with a few seconds of music in it, which I was able to "open" and "list." The hardest part was making sense of the lengthy program code, identifying the part that referred to the music, and working out the meaning of a series of statements beginning with enigmatic words.

September 29

Today I didn't have the chance to do these exercises (which, like all exercises, are best done daily) at my usual time, around noon—they're normally the first activity of the day after breakfast—and so I'm doing them on what's technically September 30, at 3 a.m. It should be understandable, then, if they don't go as well as one might hope. I'm only starting them now because once I'd finished all the tasks that prevented me from doing them at the usual time, I forgot all about them and instead sat down at the computer to continue my investigations into sound. After a while, I managed to bring about some interesting birdlike cheeping, which I recorded, though I'm still not entirely sure how I managed it. Previously, using a similar method—or perhaps the same one, since I don't remember exactly what steps I followed—I made it produce the sound of a guitar or mandolin. But I didn't record that and now it's lost, at least for the time being.

I'm still not entirely sure how sound works on the computer. I know how sound works in general, but not specific sounds, since each one involves three values—or four, if we include duration. The most disconcerting thing is that varying one of these values sometimes has the same effect as varying another. So the research goes on, the investigations go on. And for now, I have the cheeping.

September 30

Today I'm starting slightly earlier than yesterday: 10:25 p.m. But my writing's too small. Let's see: a slight effort at enlargement. That's better. Don't let it shrink again. Good. Now to concentrate on forming each letter. Forming each letter. Forming each letter. Slowly does it . . . But how the hell do you do a capital S? S. L. §. &. It's no use. I can't remember. A B C D E F G H I J K L M N O P Q R S T U V W X Y Z. Well, I don't remember the K or the S, and nor am I very confident about the Q. (Alicia's come to bother me. She's always extremely jealous of my time alone. If she sees me concentrating on something other than her she'll invariably try to distract me, making me lose my thread, my flow, and spilling my cerebral juices all over the place. In my experience, this is a universal law. In the experience of other men I know too. But I still don't fully understand it and it makes life very difficult. Really, these exercises I'm doing to strengthen my character are a clumsy substitute for literature. I thought I'd be able to write a single page like this every day with no trouble at all, but that's not what happens when Alicia's at home.)

October 1

Onward, then, with the handwriting therapy. I must confess that I've already noticed some positive psychological results, or so I believe, all related to different aspects of self-affirmation. And even if I'm wrong about this, it's still helpful to believe it. (To be honest, I can't think of a single true belief, by which I mean a belief consistent with reality, that would make much practical difference to anything. But then all beliefs are actually false, i.e., inconsistent with reality, since they're limiting, inadequate, and incapable of encompassing the rich variety of the Universe in all its dimensions. And yet precisely because they're limiting, and as long as they aren't wildly outlandish—and sometimes even if they are—beliefs can have a tangible, precise effect on everything you do. Which means that to get anywhere in life, you have to believe in something. In other words, you have to be wrong.)

Let's leave things there. I think this is doing me good, helping with my self-affirmation. I feel much cheerier as a result, and with renewed strength to go on fighting for my recovery, that thing that seems so difficult, and perhaps even impossible, to achieve. Of course, I'd make much more progress if I didn't face such stark opposition from certain factions of the world around me; I know full well that every step I take toward self-affirmation on the inside is harshly punished on the outside. But I'll keep fighting nevertheless, and I'll get there.

October 2

The problem of making sounds on the computer is still plaguing me. It's really two problems in one. First, I still don't understand the function of each of the three values governing the production of a single sound, and second, although I know how to select the notes, I can't make any real music out of them, not even a very simple melody. I'm having trouble with the rhythms, too, from both a technical and a musical point of view.

October 3

Today is not a good day. Alicia doesn't feel well, which is understandable, since her maid has just announced out of the blue that today was her last day—she's found a job in an office where she'll start out earning almost two and a half times what she's paid here. This is a real tragedy for us, comparable to the death of a relative or close friend. I hope that time, the great healer, will gradually soothe the pain of this terrible loss, though everyone knows there's not a woman alive today who can compare to our good, efficient, obedient, taciturn, sublime Antonieta.

October 4

A bad day for calligraphical exercises, and for lots of other things too. It's raining (which I enjoy, though it makes me even more inclined than usual to sleep and do nothing). Yesterday (today) I went to bed after five in the morning; at ten thirty I was woken up by a truck with loudspeakers attached, which stopped right outside our house and held forth about some stupid raffle, at great length and appalling volume. Then, without having gotten back to sleep properly—I'd been dozing, but that was it—at twelve thirty I was woken up once and for all by Juan Ignacio and his grandmother, who were shouting for the dog in a deafening chorus. Because of all this, my eyes are burning and I don't feel like doing anything. I notice, however, that except for the odd slipup, my writing is large and clear.

October 6

It's fitting and helpful to have a ritual like this, of writing first thing every day. There's something of a religious spirit about it, and you need that in life—though I've been losing it over the years for various reasons, along with Humanity as a whole. It's very irritating to be so easily influenced by, and dependent upon, a society whose opinions, motivations, aims, and beliefs I mostly don't share. But a person means so little as an isolated being, however much they've strengthened themselves as an individual and however emphatic their individualism may be. The fact is, all the individuals in the world are nothing but the crossover points between threads that stretch far beyond us, reaching from one unknown place to another. Not even this language I'm using belongs to me. I didn't invent it, and if I had it would be no use for communicating anyway.

This trivial digression was interrupted by Juan Ignacio (who's just looked over my shoulder and seen his name written down and wants to know what this is all about). (So I write: "Juan Ignacio is a fool.")

October 13

I'm a naughty boy. I haven't done my homework for days. I haven't showered for days, either. I smell terrible.

It all started when Antonieta left—our house hasn't been the same since. Not that it was ever anything special, but now it's much worse. I can't work out why this is happening. I've had maids before, at various times in my life, and their absences never particularly troubled me. They'd come once or twice a week and whisk through the work in two to three hours. My house was always reasonably clean, maybe because I'm a tidy person. Dirty dishes would pile up in the kitchen, but when they started bothering me I'd roll up my sleeves and wash them myself. The bed was never made, but I didn't mess it up much when I slept, so at night all I had to do was straighten the sheets and blankets a bit. I don't see the problem with an unmade bed or a few unwashed plates. But my opinion (that "the Sabbath was made for man, not man for the Sabbath") counts for nothing in this house; instead, we live within a rigid structure determined by Cleanliness, which has become a value more highly prized than People and Life.

October 16

Yesterday I managed only three and a half lines of exercises, and then I was interrupted and had to stop. It happened just as I was beginning to write about interruptions, or rather, about my desperate need for some continuity in my work, some order and discipline, because these mindless, scattered days aren't doing me any good. They overwhelm me, making me forget who I am and sucking the meaning out of existence.

It's not that I define myself by my work, and nor am I one of those people who can't live without something to do or even who have the capacity to get bored. No, when I talk about continuity in my work, I might just as well be talking about continuity in my free time. What matters is the continuity itself, and the psychological danger comes from fragmentation—at least, it does in my case, and in this phase of my life.

It's not interruptions or changes in activity that upset things, but rather sudden interruptions and forced changes when I haven't had the chance to complete a psychological process, whether in my work or in my leisure activities.

The situation is made worse by the accumulation of things to do, which, thanks to all the interruptions, I never get around to. Days, weeks, and months can go by like this; unfinished tasks mount up and weigh on me, and it seems impossible to get through them all—unless, as with my monthly crossword obligations, they become urgent. I live from one urgency to the next.

October 17

I've realized that the system of interruptions governing this house derives from the fact that Alicia is a fractal being (see Mandelbrot) with a fractal pattern of behavior. And since she decides what goes on in this family, everything that goes on is fractal and can develop only in a fractal way, like a snowflake.

Psychological fractility must surely correspond to some psychological fracture. I don't think these phenomena have been studied in enough detail. For now, I could formulate a kind of law to describe the general behavior of this family I find myself in: "Any movement toward a goal will immediately be diverted toward another goal, and so on, and the movement toward the original goal may or may not ever be resumed."

October 25

Today I failed in my grand plans to start living more healthily, with less time spent on things like reading and using the computer, precisely because of an irresistible urge to use the computer. There's always some idea I want to try out, or some mystery that needs solving once and for all. I think the computer is taking the place of my Unconscious as a field of investigation. I went as far as I could with my investigations into my Unconscious, and the by-product of those investigations is the literature I've written (although literature was also a tool I used in those investigations, in some cases at least).

To be honest, the world of the computer is very similar to the world of the Unconscious, with lots of hidden elements and a language to decipher. I probably feel like there's nowhere left to go when it comes to investigating my Unconscious; the computer also involves much less risk, or risk of a different kind.

The strangest thing about all this is the value I ascribe to investigating something that is, quite definitely, of no use to me whatsoever. And yet I clearly do see it as immensely valuable, as if there were vitally important clues hidden in the workings of the machine. (Once again I got distracted by the topic and paid no attention to forming the letters properly, or to the size of my writing.)

October 26

Over the past few days spring has sprung, or rather it's loudly announced its presence all over the place. Our garden is teeming with plants we didn't plant; they're popping up everywhere, apparently of their own volition or because the soil itself is feeling inspired. They develop quickly, getting bigger by the day and making themselves very much at home. There's a proliferation of insects and feverish activity among the ants. In the street the girls are blossoming too, their breasts seeming to awaken and press keenly against light fabrics that barely conceal them. They look around boldly, their eyes full of life and the pleasure of living.

My own personal spring primarily involves taking high doses of psychiatric medication in a (futile) attempt to control the usual anxiety running through my veins. The seasons are all the same in this house, each as depressingly oppressive as the last. A big invisible clock marks the same time for every day, every month, every year; it marks the rhythm of the blood in the veins, the beating of the heart, the forbidden desires, forbidden but sometimes—if the clock allows it—permitted in dribs and drabs. Life, with its own logic, its own hungers and needs, is going on somewhere, but not here. Here, all that goes on is the prisoner's unproductive solitude, the inner chill that summer will never dispel. Time doesn't run alongside us and we don't know how to play with it; time is nothing but a murderer, slow but sure, watching mockingly from behind its scythe as it lets us go on enjoying—in manageable portions—the cold that awaits us in the tomb that bears our name.

October 27

I'll make an effort to avoid interesting topics today so I can get better at forming the letters, which I've almost completely forgotten about doing. What can I write that won't be so interesting that it distracts me from my purpose and at the same time won't be so mind-numbingly dull that I wander off, yawning expansively, and leave the work half-done?

(Juan Ignacio has come to interrupt me. There's no shortage of interruptions in this house, as I think I may have mentioned before. He's asking for his mother. I tell him she's not here.) (But I'm not going to write about interruptions, despite the fact that at this very moment someone is ringing the doorbell.) (Juan Ignacio comes in and asks about his mother again, not for himself this time but on behalf of the man who rang the bell, as if my answer were going to be any different. "She's not here.") (But as I was saying, I'm not going to discuss interruptions now. They affect me directly and are the main cause of my sorry psychological state, which makes them an interesting topic, and I resolved at the beginning of today's work to avoid interesting topics. Although uninteresting topics also conspire against my handwriting—but for a different reason, of course.)

October 28

On I go, trying to write about uninteresting things, perhaps heralding a new era of boredom as a literary movement. Today I started out with very big writing, which after just two lines has already reduced considerably in size. Why was that? Because I began thinking about how to finish my sentence, wanting to be sure it made sense. Conclusion: I'm incapable of paying attention—what little attention I have—to more than one thing at a time. Here, the priority is the handwriting and not the prose, which means that making no sense is perfectly acceptable. So stop worrying and start forming those letters, boy: nose to the grindstone. It's not easy to get used to the idea of not making sense. Although, really, sense is nothing but a complicated social construct. I suspect that last sentence is entirely untrue, but I can't let myself start philosophizing now, about that or anything else. I have to concentrate on my handwriting; that's the point of all this. I have to let my inner self change and grow under the magical influence of graphology. Big writing, big me. Small writing, small me. Beautiful writing, beautiful me.

November 2

It's been a few days since I last did these graphological exercises, but there are good reasons for that: whether because of circumstances or because the exercises are working, lately I've been feeling motivated to do other things. The most important of these things, at least in my eyes, is the half-dreaming, half-waking, and almost subterranean task of trying to revive my imaginative abilities and therefore my writing. In practice, this has simply meant making the final revisions to a short story I wrote some years ago, putting it in an envelope, and sending it off to see if anyone wants to publish it. I've also been busy in the field of international relations, catching up with some correspondents abroad, and this involved the far-from-easy (in Colonia) task of getting ahold of some good-quality photocopies. What would have been wrapped up within a couple of hours in a civilized place, here required three days.

My handwriting's terrible today, more of an agitated scrawl. It's intelligible, however, and many of the features I've been trying to improve are now there without my having to think about them. Some need more work, though. That's why I have to keep writing slowly about uninteresting things: so that through patient repetition my writing develops the characteristics I think it needs in order to be completely legible again, and so that, in parallel, my behavior develops the characteristics this new, hypothetically acceptable handwriting would reveal in a graphological examination. And then I could declare myself "the artist of my own destiny." This may be a rather grandiose ambition, but sometimes it's no bad thing to aim high, especially in a field where everything colludes to make you aim low, and where mediocrity is what really impresses people.

November 13

You'll have seen (and I said "You" because I need to practice my capital Y's) how effective I'm finding these exercises as a way of settling the mind and readying it for the day ahead. Because of this, it's a serious error to begin the day with any other kind of work (those infernal crosswords, for instance) and leave these wholesome exercises for a future moment, which sometimes never comes, or comes too late.

There was a time, not so long ago, when my daily handwriting exercises seemed on the verge of becoming literary exercises instead. I was very tempted to turn my calligraphical prose into narrative prose, with the idea of building a series of texts that, like the steps of a staircase, would carry me back up to those longed-for heights I was once able to reach. But the Devil invariably sticks his hoof in. He's always crouching out of sight somewhere, peering into the heart of Man, and he chose that moment to dangle a (temporary) job in front of me that would help me save up some money—something I needed to do to stay on top of things, clear my debts, and be left with a reassuring sum in my pocket. So I took the job, and that was the end of my resolve to write, and even, for a few days, of these exercises. Coming back to them now, I once again feel the urge to write something. To write and be published. I need to see my name in print—my real name, the one I use when I write, and not the one I was given. And more, much more, than that, I want to get in touch with myself, with the miraculous being that lives inside me and is able, among so many other extraordinary things, to fabricate interesting stories and cartoons. That's the point. That's what it's all about. Reconnecting with the inner being, the being which is part, in some secret way, of the divine spark that roams tirelessly through the Universe, giving it life, keeping it going, and lending reality to what would otherwise be an empty shell.

November 15

I'm going to try using these exercises to settle my mind, readying it for the day ahead (which is shaping up to be a tough one, though you can never tell with these things: yesterday, for example, everything was shaping up swimmingly until the neighbors informed me that Ignacio was on his way home from school because he'd been feeling ill. That destroyed my peace and quiet for the rest of the day and for today as well, days that had been marked out for the most absolute and glorious solitude, since there was a school trip scheduled. And so Ignacio—who, by the way, is feeling perfectly fine—is at home, in bed out of laziness and his own free will, calling me into his room every so often just to exert his control over me and make me feel his power, and because his mother is in Caracas I have to obey, fussing over him guiltily the way invalids always make you).

November 20

Let's see if I can pull myself together enough today to form the letters properly. I woke up this morning feeling distinctly ill at ease with myself. As far as I can tell, this is because for too long now—too many years—I've been living outside myself, concerned only with what's going on around me. And on the rare occasions when I've been able to turn my gaze inward, I've connected not with the most substantial parts of myself but with the most trivial, "subconscious" ones. What's happened to my soul? Where has it gone? For ages, as I said to Alicia awhile ago, I've been in a bad way because I have no connection to eternity. I meant that I'm seeing things superficially, that my experiences are shallow, that I'm a long way from my Inner Self; too far, and with no idea of the possible routes back. It doesn't matter what happens to you if you've been separated from Yourself; everything's equally weightless and goes by without leaving a trace.

The problem isn't the demands of the outside world, even though I often think it is, but rather my attachment, or commitment, to those demands.

I need to give this more thought.

November 21

Since my handwriting has received justifiable criticism of late, today I'm doing my best to produce a script that's elegant, svelte, large, and easy to read. There's something really nefarious about the weather here in Colonia, and it sends the nervous system into disarray. Today I got up early and went out to run some errands before noon, and (speaking of "svelte" handwriting) my body felt monstrous and muddled, as if I'd turned into a kind of toad with a disgusting swollen belly, dragging myself laboriously along on weak, stubby legs. Walking three or four blocks through the town in this cloying, stormy weather is a herculean task. Despair clings to your skin like the sticky heat. All you can think about is finding a dark, cool place where you can lie down and let life pass you by. As Juan Ignacio says, "It's a struggle."

But I'm no longer trying my best when it comes to my handwriting. Instead, I'm getting carried away by the subject matter and forgetting about forming the letters. I can't concentrate on both things at once. That's better; now I'm thinking only about the letters. Which means I won't attempt to do anything other than form them properly. No letting in other thoughts that have nothing to do with the business of forming letters. It's boring. I can't think of anything to write, like a person who can't think of anything to say when someone thrusts a microphone in their face and demands a comment. It seems that the function of writing or talking depends entirely on meaning, on thought, and you can't think consciously about thinking itself. Similarly, you can't write for the sake of writing, or think for the sake of thinking, without meaning being involved.

November 22

Yesterday I noticed that the days when I have messy handwriting are also the days when I smoke considerably more cigarettes than usual. Conclusion: bad handwriting is caused by anxiety. Now I just have to work out what causes the anxiety, but that will be much easier to do thanks to a dream I had the other day. The dream, or part of the dream, involved a vague narrative relating to a war and various soldiers or policemen I had to hide from. But the main story line was about some bicycles my parents were thinking of selling, which belonged to me.

(Several interruptions—in real life, not in the dream. The psychologist turned up unexpectedly to see a patient in the consulting room she shares with Alicia; the dog followed her in, as did her son—the psychologist's son, I mean—who she'd brought along for Ignacio to entertain. Ignacio tried to escape, but it was too late, and now he's entertaining him. Then the architect arrived, which meant the dog came in again, after all my efforts to get him back outside. The architect had some new plans and quotes with her for the house we've just bought. Things are getting more complicated by the day.)

They were my bicycles, and I was upset that my parents were selling them.

November 23

No stone is left unturned in this house when it comes to my entertainment or amusement (whether I like it or not). For example, today Alicia thought she'd soak one of Juan Ignacio's overalls in a bucket of soapy water. She left the bucket in the kitchen, under the window, between some chairs and the electric stove. A few hours later, when I was in the kitchen having a cup of coffee and trying to read a chapter of my detective novel, Ignacio came over for a chat (he does that a lot these days, generally to discuss matters relating somehow or other to sex). He sat sideways on one of the chairs in his casual, nonchalant way, resting one foot on the rim of the bucket. He has a tendency to fidget restlessly when he's speaking, and with one of his movements his foot slipped off the rim of the bucket and into the water, knocking the whole thing over. I still can't understand how, if Ignacio then stood up and his leg was more or less vertical, or diagonal at any rate, the bucket could have ended up completely overturned with Juan Ignacio's leg still inside it. He couldn't extract his leg any more than he could set the bucket upright, and so he simply watched, transfixed, as the bucket's entire contents emptied spectacularly onto the floor. The whole kitchen was flooding, and I hastily retreated to a strategic location with my book, my reading glasses, and my cup of coffee; in other words, I went into my study. When Alicia came back, and after her fury and despair had subsided, another scene played out that was even more comical than the last. As Alicia set to work drying the floor, Ignacio and I leaned comfortably in the kitchen doorway, watching her exertions with great interest. It didn't occur to us that we were doing anything wrong until Alicia shot us a murderous glance, and then the whole scene suddenly struck me as hilarious. After moving prudently out of her reach, I began roaring with laughter.

November 25

I'm fully aware that these exercises are becoming less calligraphical and more literary as time goes on; there's a discourse—a style, a form, more than an idea—that won't leave me alone, and it's getting the better of me. The blank page is like a big chocolate pudding; I'm not allowed to eat it because I'm on a diet, but I can't resist. And although technically nothing and no one is stopping me from writing whatever I want, however I want, and although I have reams of blank paper I could use for one sort of writing <u>and</u> the other, there's a strange factor at play, which it would be too easy to label the "time factor" (it's more of an "anxiety factor," and even if anxiety and time have always been closely related, they're different things). There is, I was saying, a strange factor in all this that's pushing me to superimpose one kind of writing onto the other, which means I don't succeed at either because the result is stuck somewhere between the two. But this strange factor that I'm calling <u>anxiety</u>: where does it come from? The first explanation that occurs to me, which I therefore suspect of being superficial, is that I feel the handwriting exercises are "allowed" in a way the narrative ones aren't. So the discourse emerges, struggling against its own suppression, and the result of this face-off between writer and superego is as frustrating as any other transaction you can't control, like an erotic dream that ends in veiled, symbolic images, gaps in the story line, and infinite delay.

There you have it: for years I've been delaying the free narrative act indefinitely, with one excuse or another. And it's not that I find it hard to let go of the idea of writing; most of the time I'm not even conscious of wanting to write, but then I feel driven to as soon as I pick up my pen and face the blank page.

Part Two: The Empty Discourse

The Discourse

November 25, 1990

There's a flow, a rhythm, a seemingly empty form; the discourse could end up addressing any topic, image, or idea. This indifference makes me suspicious. I suspect there are all kinds of things—too many—lurking behind the apparent emptiness. I've never found emptiness particularly frightening; sometimes it's even been a place of refuge. What I find frightening is not being able to escape this rhythm, this form that flows onward without revealing its contents. That's why I've decided to write this, beginning with the form, with the flow itself, and introducing the problem of emptiness as its subject matter. I hope that this way I'll gradually discover the real subject matter, which for now is disguised as emptiness.

I don't want to force things with images from the past or explanations of the present, which always sound false. I'd rather let the form itself speak, so it reveals its contents bit by bit of its own accord. However, I can't reveal that I'm waiting for it to give something away, because that would send it slipping straight back into apparent emptiness again. I need to be alert but with my eyes half-closed, as if I were thinking about something else entirely and had no interest in the discourse taking shape. It's like climbing into a fish tank and waiting for the waters to settle and the fish to forget they had ever been disturbed, so they move closer, their curiosity drawing them toward me and toward the surface of the tank. Then I'll be able to see them—and perhaps even catch one.

What I can't do is imagine a reader other than myself—I'd be afraid of boring anyone else with page after page of nothing, of subjecting them to my dissimulated waiting game, my somewhat interpretative approach to revealing the form. Perhaps a reader who isn't me would already have found something of the true content of the discourse in these lines. The thought of this alarms me even more than the thought of being boring. How humiliating to give myself away to the reader before I've given anything away to myself, blissfully unaware that anything's been given away at all! And by now something almost certainly has. For a start, this image that's arisen of a hypothetical reader who's more perceptive than I am strikes me as very paranoid. The discourse is revealing its paranoid side. Well, I suppose that's something. But I worry that this discovery, which tells me nothing about the contents of the discourse, has sent the fish in the tank shooting off in all directions.

Let's wait a bit. Think of a distraction. Since it's difficult not to talk about anything, the best approach would be to distract the discourse by filling it up with trivial things, things that have nothing to do with the matter at hand and don't so much as allude to my distraction-related tactics. I need to turn my gaze away from the discourse and onto some insignificant alternative topic. It's up to me to choose one. I could, for example, talk about the weather (which would have the advantage of getting rid of the hypothetical other reader, the one who's more perceptive than me, once and for all).

But I've just been interrupted by the phone. I answered it because I'm at home alone and thought it might be for me, but, as usual, it was for Alicia. These interruptions in my activities are all too common. Until now, I've almost always lived alone and interruption-free. These days I live with a woman, a child, a dog, and a cat (and a maid, who comes every morning from Monday to Saturday; now it's a Sunday afternoon). The dog and the cat spend their time in the back garden and are fairly easygoing; any problems between them tend to arise at mealtimes. The dog has a far longer history in the house than the cat. The cat is a recent addition, mysterious, white-furred, and very guarded with his emotions, though very rash, or perhaps oblivious, when it comes to other kinds of danger. Ever since the arrival of the cat, the dog has been seized by jealousy.

Exercises

November 27

Allow me to record, so it's known in the centuries to come, that I'm writing this at eight thirty in the morning. If we take into account the clocks going forward (a maneuver on the part of the government that I still don't understand, though I'm sure it leaves them better off and us worse off), it's 7:30 a.m. I've already had breakfast and now I'm drinking a cup of coffee. But my handwriting isn't very good. Now it is. If I want my handwriting to be good, I can write only about my handwriting, which becomes very monotonous. But writing only about my handwriting keeps my mind on what I'm doing and means I form the letters properly. Otherwise, my attention drifts toward the discourse, and my hand ends up writing automatically, without any will to guide it.

The will: this is the crux of my current problem. I seem to have lost my willpower—which, by the way, I never had much of. Let's think about this. The self is defined as the conscious, volitional part of the being—it's a complex modern invention, since for millennia there was nothing among living beings that bore the slightest resemblance to a self. In other words, for the being it takes real effort, a significant consumption of mental energy, to maintain the existence of this unnatural, antinatural artifice. Well, I'm doing a good job of identifying my current problem of apathy, but not such a good job of paying attention to my handwriting—I got too excited about these psychological reflections, and now my hand's moving mechanically, automatically, without a will to control it.

The Discourse

November 27

In fact, the dog also predates me in this house, and in this family. I, like the cat, am a relative newcomer. My arrival meant a number of changes for the dog, some for the better and others less so, and I have no idea what the final balance is (though I'd like to think it's worked out very well for him overall). The dog used to live permanently in our spacious back garden, which is enclosed by a high wall, a hedge, and a wire fence: escape was impossible. He spent most of the day with his paws resting on the fence, looking at the outside world and barking when he thought it necessary. On the street corner, separated from the back garden by the wire fence, there's an empty lot surrounded by low, crumbling walls. This lot is often visited by children, adults, and animals, some of which would rouse the dog's baser instincts and send him into fits of furious, insistent barking, and since barking alone wasn't enough to use up all the energy his instincts unleashed, he'd also run around, sometimes in circles and sometimes in a straight line up and down the length of the fence. He reacted in a similar way to things that happened in the road or on the opposite pavement, a world he knew only by sight and, to a certain extent, but only to a certain extent, by smell. The sense of sight doesn't mean much to dogs; I imagine the world looks to them like a sort of fuzzy black-and-white film, or the shadows in "The Allegory of the Cave" (see Plato). A dog needs to see things, but most of all he needs to smell things, and smell them up close, at that. Sometimes he even needs to touch them. Although dogs' hearing is extremely sharp, its main purpose seems to be defensive, and I don't suppose it adds a great deal to their vital, aesthetic perception of reality.

The dog, then, was a prisoner. At night he was chained up for shadowy reasons I never heard convincingly explained, and at night he also did a lot of barking, or dragged his chains around on the paving stones, or sent his bucket of water crashing over and then pushed it about with his nose.

Even before I installed myself in this house—which we'll very soon be leaving—I was worried about the dark, restricted life the poor animal led. The first thing I did on moving in was restrict it even further, since the barking under the bedroom window at night, combined with the ghostly rattling of the chain and the overturned water bucket, was disturbing my sleep. We agreed to move the kennel to the outdoor courtyard at the center of the house, thus separating the dog from the goings-on in the street and the empty lot, and these days we put him there every night before bed. This has worked well. The dog now sleeps peacefully, except sometimes when there's a full moon and choruses of dogs strike up in the small hours for mysterious reasons I wish I understood, and our dog joins in with his distinctive, familiar voice. But most of the time he sleeps peacefully at night, and so do I.

The next step was to take charge of his food. He used to be fed just once a day, which meant he was putting on a lot of weight. I started splitting his meals into smaller portions, which is proven to help with weight loss, and this forged a special bond between us: I became *the person who feeds him*, an extremely important role in the eyes of a dog, and worthy of the greatest respect and admiration—or at least, that's what people say. I think it's more that the dog sees me as one of his employees, and sometimes I even get the feeling he's watching me closely and weighing how useful I really am.

I was still worried about his lack of freedom and the limited scope of his world, and one day I had the idea of gradually widening a gap in the wire fence, or rather a gap between the iron post holding up one end of the fence and the wall it was leaning against and attached to at various points. What I did was separate the post from the wall a little at a time: if the dog really wanted to get out, I thought, at some point he'd realize he could use that gap, and it wouldn't take much effort to widen it enough to fit through. I didn't want to take all the initiative; I thought he should win his freedom for himself, because, as I know all too well, the only true freedom is the kind you win for yourself. At the same time, granting the dog his freedom involved accepting some degree of responsibility for it. I didn't want to be implicated in anything that might happen when the dog, so unfamiliar with the wider world, was first able to move freely within it. Often, at night, I've suffered in silence as visions of the dog under the wheels of a passing car danced before my eyes. I wanted him to share at least some of that responsibility with me by widening the gap in the fence himself. I'd given him the idea; he had to be the one to carry it out.

Exercises

November 28

Yesterday I began discussing an interesting topic, and now I can't remember what it was, which can only be good news for these handwriting exercises. As I recall, I'd been writing away neatly and patiently until the interesting topic came up, and then any attempt to form the letters properly fell by the wayside. I hope nothing interesting comes up today. It seems unlikely that anything will. Although I got up later than I did yesterday I'm still half-asleep, as if I could have done with a few more hours, and I feel physically exhausted. Maybe I'm having some sort of hepatic or digestive crisis. I'm in that alert, irritable state that makes me oversensitive to sudden noises or movements; it's a kind of half-awakeness, as if a part of me—and an important part, at that—is asleep and the small part that's conscious is busy, among other things, protecting the part that's still snoozing. As a result, I have a very short attention span and not much energy for practical tasks like this. And although no interesting topics have come up, my handwriting was getting progressively worse until four lines ago, when I realized and started trying to do a bit better, with some success. Thankfully, I'm now reaching the end of the page. I hope I'm feeling better when I come back to this work tomorrow.

The Discourse

November 28

The discourse, then, has been filling up with the story of the dog. It's false content, or perhaps semi-false, since, like all things, it could easily be seen as symbolic of other, deeper things. In fact, I think it would be difficult for the content of anyone's words—unless that person is a politician—for the content of any ordinary, honestly spoken words, to be false.

This doesn't mean that the abstract form of my discourse, its rhythm and flow, is determined by the story of the dog. It's more that the story of the dog could be a symbol of the real contents of the discourse, which for some reason it's impossible to see directly.

For example, it could be that the gap in the wire fence I'm gradually widening in the story corresponds to another, psychological gap, which I'm also gradually widening with some kind of freedom in mind, not the dog's freedom this time but my own. In other words, something within me is working away, secretly and slowly, to penetrate defenses that have long been erected inside me, a wall built just as secretly and slowly to protect me from something—and that may be why I'm writing this now. Though of course, even if these walls are fairly useful at the time, they eventually end up imprisoning the spirit.

And now that I think, and write, about all this, I remember an example from a few years ago, a time when I put up a defensive wall not at all secretly or slowly, but rather entirely deliberately. Or at least I think it was deliberate. I was conscious of doing it, I mean, but perhaps I didn't have a choice. Perhaps that thing hidden inside me gave the command, and the command reached my consciousness, which then acted upon it as if it had originated there. I'm thinking of the day—March 5, 1985, to be precise—when I left my old apartment in the center of Montevideo and got into the car of some friends, which was going to take me to Buenos Aires. I was moving there permanently, or so I thought. The permanence of the change may not have been definite or absolute when it came to Buenos Aires, but it was when it came to leaving my apartment, on which an eviction notice had been served. As I shut the door for the last time, I knew I would never live there again. And I'd lived there, for better or worse, for 80 percent of the forty-five years I'd been alive at the time I got into the car.

November 29

And so, by using the image of the dog to fill the empty, or seemingly empty, discourse, I've discovered that the apparent emptiness was hiding some painful content. It's pain I chose not to feel at the time because I knew I couldn't cope with it, or at least because I knew I was too busy to release it little by little in a way that would make it bearable. Because on March 5, 1985, in the early afternoon, I got into the car that was to take me to Buenos Aires "permanently," and on March 6, 1985, at ten o'clock in the morning, I was due to start work in an office in Buenos Aires. And I was going to have to adjust to life in a different city, a different country. There was no time to feel the pain of all this, so I opted to anesthetize myself instead.

This anesthesia was a conscious psychological act. At the time I called it "pulling down the shutters," and a little later "controlled psychosis": a denial operation that essentially involved telling myself over and over, "I don't mind about leaving all this," "I'm quite happy to be leaving all this: this city that oppressed me and that I saw destroyed during the dictatorship years; this apartment where I've lived, suffered, and loved; these friends who used the apartment as a meeting place, and almost a place for therapy." I didn't use words to say it, but rather a mental process I don't know how to describe; something like blocking channels, disconnecting wires, and erecting barricades between myself and every emotion that threatened to take shape. I knew it wasn't true, that I did mind, that I wasn't happy. What I was happy about, though, was the prospect of starting a new life and having new experiences at an age when I hadn't been expecting a great deal to change.

Until then, I'd seen my life as a finished work—not finished to my satisfaction, perhaps, but without anything major on the horizon. I'd spent the year before carefully preparing myself for death. And although my clinical death didn't come after all, the spiritual death that came in its place never really left, though I don't like to say so, and will perhaps be hanging around until my clinical death, though I don't like to say that either. But the possibility of change meant the possibility of life, and I had to be very brave, and to do that I had to be very desperate, since I thought I no longer had the energy for any kind of change at all. Making those particular changes seemed quite impossible, and it took real courage to embark on them. I needed all my reserves of psychological energy, as well as rigorous self-discipline and a steely resistance to fear. I couldn't let myself be afraid, any more than I could let myself look over my shoulder at the things I was leaving behind.

Exercises

November 30

I went to bed late last night (at 4:00 a.m.) and woke up late today, aching all over. I have lots of work to do, and I've also managed to track down the LOGO handbook; because of all this, I'm not expecting much from today's exercises. And I see my writing's coming out very small, probably because I'm feeling guilty. Things aren't going well. Whatever's happening inside and around me seems to slide far too easily into chaos. It's true, I know, that I should be more resilient and not get drawn into the madness of my surroundings, but it's also true that I'm used to having more control over my surroundings than I do now. And I can never work out how to separate myself from the world around me, however much people talk about my "ivory tower." I'm too aware of everything that's going on. For one thing, I find it impossible to get into bed, close my eyes, and fall asleep if I know other people in the house are still up. This is because the other people in the house cannot be trusted. If Ignacio's awake, for example, he'll definitely fall asleep with both the TV and his bedroom light on. And I can't rely on Alicia to switch off the television or the light while I'm asleep, especially if she's already in bed, because she too has a tendency to doze off inadvertently, without the slightest concern for whatever else might be going on. It's also unlikely she'll remember to take out the trash, turn off the lights, close the windows and lower the blinds in her office, lock the front door with the key rather than the bolt and make sure the doormat is blocking the gap underneath it, put the food in the fridge, set her alarm, and, most importantly, refrain from making any noise once I've fallen asleep.

The Discourse

November 30

But I might as well go on with the story of the dog and the cat. I still don't feel ready to delve too deeply into those painful episodes from my past, especially considering that my "voluntary psychosis" was taking root and becoming less and less voluntary as the months and years went by. These days I find returning to the past extremely hard work; I'm not even sure I can do it. Nor am I sure that this is what the discourse is really about; there could be plenty of other things still concealed within it, and in fact, I'd say there definitely are. But I have no great passion for psychoanalysis, and it would be enough to reveal a moderate amount of what's behind the apparent emptiness without having to go back to the original causes of everything, which are almost certainly preverbal.

The dog, then, remained indifferent to the hole in his fence as I widened it gradually each day. Or perhaps it never occurred to him that he could escape through it, or it occurred to him but seemed too risky to attempt. About a month passed before he finally decided to wriggle into the space between the metal post and the wall and loosen the post a little more, just a little, so he could get out into the empty lot on the other side. It was being in heat that made him do it. (People have argued with me before about the matter of male dogs being in heat, and I don't want to reopen that controversy now. It could be that what I call "heat" in my dog is a response to a female dog in the area actually being in heat. But whatever it is, it involves a radical change in a male dog's behavior.)

When a dog is in heat, as I soon found out, his personality is completely different. He becomes euphoric, manic, and more aggressive and impulsive than usual. And so, one afternoon, the dog slipped through to the other side of the wire fence as if it were the easiest thing in the world. He sniffed around the empty lot for a while with a combination of delight and profound interest, like a true professional, uncovering who knows how many hidden stories—the kind of stories that can be revealed to dogs only by their scents and will be forever unknown to humans if we aren't there to see them take place. I'm convinced the dog can interpret smells, translating them into a full understanding of the events that generated them. We humans are limited to very basic associations, for example when we open a drawer for the first time in ages and catch the fleeting aroma of an old perfume, which had until then been clinging to the fabric of some clothes. The scent stimulates the memory, but it doesn't tell us anything new.

On one of these days, I saw the dog step impulsively through the door into the back garden and use his sense of smell to reconstruct an entire scene that had played out between the cat and myself a few minutes before: the cat following me over the paving stones, rubbing against my legs; me retracing my steps back into the house with the cat at my side; me going out again with a few pieces of meat, and the cat nibbling on them serenely by the door. The dog followed each one of these movements, in the correct order and with absolute precision, and I could see from the expression on his face that he was drawing conclusions.

But I'm getting ahead of myself by introducing the cat. I was supposed to be telling the story of the dog's first outing into the wider world, or at least his first independent outing. Before that, every now and then, though not very often, he'd been driven to the beach with his chain around his neck, the same one we used to chain him up at night when his kennel was still in the back garden.

December 3

I just read through everything I've written so far in one sitting, which gave rise to a flurry of associations and emotions—so many that now I feel stuck again, as if I'm standing at a crossroads and unsure which way to go. Even though I know that any direction would be much the same as any other, since my original aim hasn't changed: I still want to capture the content hidden behind the apparent emptiness of the discourse. I'm not in a hurry to do this, or at least I shouldn't be. But I can feel myself getting more anxious by the day, at a rate I could even represent graphically by means of a curve showing my daily intake of cigarettes. The root of this anxiety is probably the feeling that there's never enough time. If I ask myself why I don't have enough time at this point in my life, I'd have to give two reasons: firstly, that I've taken on too many responsibilities (to which I should add that I've also acquired many more distractions); and secondly, that my body has grown much more demanding with age (and, paradoxically, it's largely the demands of my aging body that have obliged me to accept more responsibilities).

Because these days my body needs more looking after than before, when it was sturdier and I could subject it to greater privation and strain. Looking after it costs money, to earn money it's necessary to accept responsibilities, and these responsibilities take up time. But I've also acquired new commitments for other reasons—love, for example.

For a while now, what I've been trying to do is get through all the work I've accumulated so I can accumulate some proper free time instead. Recently, though, I've realized this is the wrong strategy, that it's based on a misconception. That I've put the cart in front of the horse. You can't arrive at free time by doing more things, because everything you do leads to more things to do, and before you know it you're trapped in an interminable tangle of minor everyday oppressions. It would be better to draw a nice simplifying line between the essential and the nonessential tasks and then do no more than the absolute minimum of the nonessential ones.

But that makes me feel uneasy, too, for reasons I don't fully understand. Perhaps, it occurs to me now, because the things on the "nonessential" side of the line are themselves also essential, only on a deeper and less rational level. And now my discourse seems to have become tangled as well, and what's more, Alicia's just come back from her errands with some important things to tell me. Maybe it's for the best, though; maybe this interruption will release me from the tangle of the discourse.

Exercises

December 4

I'm making myself prioritize these exercises today, despite the psychological pressure I feel to do other, more urgent, work. Although really, trying to be more diligent about these exercises than I have been is itself a way of prioritizing urgent, profitable things above all else. Fundamentally, it's a battle to recover my identity and principles at a time of great upheaval. I can't let the whirlwind carry me away. This whirlwind, if I'm not mistaken, began with the moment the keys to the new house were handed over, or perhaps before, with the search for a new house and the decision to buy the one we eventually bought. But back then it was less a whirlwind than a few strongish gusts; only when we took possession of the new keys did the real maelstrom begin. I think it's caused, essentially, by the interaction of two personalities as different as Alicia's and my own. My character obliges me, and enables me, to do things one way and not another. I approach tasks with a degree of Zen: as far as I'm concerned, things should be done when they're good and ready, and their readiness is something I need to feel coming from within myself. I think there's a right time for everything, which arises from mysterious external causes and/or an internal event that follows a long and equally internal process of elaboration. There comes a point when you inevitably see, feel, sense, and know how things should be done, and at that precise moment you're given the strength to do them. Alicia, meanwhile, takes the opposite approach, which I'd describe as a "lack of respect for things." She believes in getting things done through sheer willpower, regardless of circumstances (external or internal), come what may.

(second sheet)

I'll go on exploring this topic while I wait for my visitor to arrive. I don't want to get caught up in any of my more complicated work, which would be more annoying to interrupt.

There's no denying that Alicia's approach makes her a lot more efficient than me. I'm often jealous of how easy she seems to find it to solve impossible problems. And yet, from the times in my life when I've taken a similar approach and acted as efficiently, I've learned that such practical efficiency can come at a high spiritual cost.

. . . *(interruption)* . . .

The efficient approach to getting things done involves over-developing the practical part of the brain, in a kind of militarization of the self. Problems become enemies to confront (and ultimately destroy), not friends to incorporate. They have to be faced head-on and resolved, not in the way that naturally suits each problem but in the way that seems "to me" to be the quickest, most economical, and most convenient at the time. There's a certain lack of respect for the problem, like the lack of respect people show nature by pruning a tree into a geometric shape.

This behavior is no good for the spirit, and neither, in the long run, is it truly efficient. We cut the thread instead of patiently untangling the knot, which means we can't use it again afterwards. The practical approach irritates the Zen approach and vice versa. Alicia and I, then, are in a constant state of mutual irritation. Things get done any old how, and in the end neither of us is even sure how we should be doing them. Alicia thinks we should move as soon as possible, and I think we should move under the best possible conditions, and this conflict is creating the whirlwind.

The Discourse

December 4

What freed me from the tangled discourse in the end was another commotion in Argentina. I was able to watch this one on television, even from outside the country (though admittedly we're not very far away). I spent hours staring at the TV screen, transfixed by the processions of tanks and the sound of gunshots of different calibers ringing out in those surroundings I know and love.

The discourse itself didn't change, but it disappeared for a while. And today I'm starting again, with nothing, remembering only very hazily that at some point I have to be brave enough to explore the "controlled psychosis" cordoning off the Montevidean 80 percent of my life from the rest of it, and feeling, equally hazily, that there's another more recent and in no way controlled psychosis to explore relating to the four years I spent living in Buenos Aires, which I've also erased from my affective memory. What percentage of me is going to be left?

* * *

An interruption, per usual. But this time it's a meaningful interruption, a kind of intrusion of my own discourse into the absence of discourse, into the nothingness of today. Alicia's just come into the house, dragging the dog behind her and muttering under her breath. She shuts him in the courtyard "in disgrace" and then announces very angrily that he's just killed a bird.

Exercises

December 5

The harder I try to stay sane, to keep myself as whole as possible in the midst of the whirlwind, the harder Alicia works to make the whirlwind more intense. She's attacking from all sides.

She decided to buy a house and set her heart on a far more expensive one than she could afford at the time. I found myself chained to my work as a crossword-setter, which is paid in dollars, as a way of helping with the debt. Meanwhile, fairly predictably, my work got more complicated thanks to some materials that needed preparing in advance, since the people I work with are on holiday in January. My work is generally more complicated these days, too, in that I've agreed to write some articles for a newspaper, which pays better than the other things I do. On top of that, there's a good chance I'm going to have a couple of books published. And on top of that, I want to write something literary rather than profitable. But the thing is, none of this seems to be enough. Not only did Alicia choose (with my approval, I should add) the particularly expensive house, but she also wants to move into it as soon as possible—ideally by the end of the year. And that's still not enough: she's also making a whole string of demands that involve a whole string of things being done to the house before we move in. She's delegated responsibility for all of this to me, wanting me to take it as a sign of trust. When I try to do things my way, however, she thinks I'm wasting time and starts doing them herself. Then she "asks for help" with the messes she gets into, and I feel myself getting worse and worse, more and more blocked and useless and with more and more to do, and all the while time is passing, dispersing into a mist in which nothing is ever resolved. I become stricter and more authoritarian, fighting to maintain some semblance of a psychological structure. But the whirlwind is gathering speed, and it's carrying me away.

The Discourse

December 5

Over the past few years, I've noticed time and again that whenever I begin writing a text like this one, which I started several days ago, something bird-related takes place. It happened twice in Buenos Aires, and it happened here in Colonia last year, when I began a short story (which I later finished, and then burned on the stove). And the other day, just as I was drifting away from the story of the dog, a bird made a dramatic entrance inside the dog's mouth. Things like this are disconcerting and troublesome, most of all because of their symbolic power. It's as if circumstances had suddenly placed me smack in the middle of a topic I'm trying to avoid, a topic I still don't feel mature enough to address.

When I started writing this, my idea was simply to recover the form of an existing discourse and wait for its contents to be revealed as I went along. Now, though, it looks as if just by beginning to write—and not for the first time—I've inadvertently come up against a secret mechanism, a secret way things have of working, and my clumsy fingers bashing away at the typewriter keys have somehow interfered with it. I feel trapped inside a mechanism I know nothing about, gripped by the magical fear that my apparently private, personal, and innocent act has put me in touch with a formidable and dangerous world, a world I can't control and can only barely, uncertainly, feel is there.

That section of my past, to which I still haven't managed to restore the emotional charge, goes on pressuring me from the hidden recesses of my unconscious. Meanwhile, my external reality is also pressuring me more and more, to work, to act, to do all kinds of things I don't want to do. I'm trapped between two worlds, which ceaselessly call to me like two gaping, insatiable mouths. For too long now I've been unable to pay enough attention to one of the mouths, and when you don't pay it enough attention, it ends up wanting to devour everything. I need to stand firm and decide what my priorities are: the most important thing has to be the inner self, the intimate call, the release of those frozen, and perhaps even slightly rotten, feelings. But I'm scared to face up to the task. I don't know how to go about it; I haven't got time to stop and look carefully into myself. And I'm frightened of getting lost for too long in that world of shadows, false pretenses, and old pain.

Exercises

December 6

The person writing these lines is the beginning of the new ME. Last night, when I was undressing for the shower, I saw an image of myself in the little bathroom mirror that I didn't like one bit. "I hate this body," I thought. Then I realized that I don't hate this fat, misshapen body because it's fat and misshapen, but instead that my body has become this way precisely because I've been hating it for so long. I realized that hating it will never help me to reshape it the way I'd like, and I also thought that being this physically monstrous must be an accurate reflection of how psychologically monstrous I am. "I need to change, body and soul," I told myself then.

When I woke up this morning, I hadn't forgotten or even broken off from this line of thinking. And I'd made a resolution—not a very clear one, admittedly, though the underlying attitude is clear enough.

The general line of thinking is this: (1) I'm too focused on what's happening around me and have lost all contact with myself; (2) My violent assault on my body and mind has been going on for too long now (the first cigarette of the day when I don't even feel like it, "to wake myself up"; the first meal of the day when I'm not even hungry, out of habit; and so on. I need to "eat when I'm hungry and sleep when I'm tired"); (3) Everything I have to do can be put off indefinitely; what I can't put off any longer is taking care of myself.

That's the general idea, and I'd like to be able to develop it further. It's very Zen, very antianxiety. But it won't be easy, because the Devil sometimes works in league with a person I love. I hope I'll be strong enough.

December 7

My perception of my body is an age-old problem. It began with my enforced immobility between the ages of three and eight or nine, during which time I learned to separate myself from my body and live in my head. Other incidents later on complicated things further, and every so often I find myself "living in my head" for extended periods of time. When I do, it's as if the body exists only when it hurts, and even then I know I have plenty of tricks to avoid feeling pain. For example, when I spend a long time reading the way I did last night, I don't notice the aches and cramps of prolonged bad posture until the moment I put the book down. Then I feel guilty—because of how late it's gotten, because I know I'll be tired and sore when I wake up, because my sight's getting worse by the day and now my eyes are weepy with exhaustion, and above all because I can tell I've fallen into that particular kind of trance that comes from lacking the willpower to change. Is it really too late to turn things around? I don't think I have much in the way of inner resources at the moment. I could do with some of that famous "motivation," but sadly I can't find any inside myself, and there's no point expecting it to come from anywhere else.

December 8

Today I read a newspaper article about the "disease of the nineties": chronic fatigue syndrome (CFS). I may not have all the symptoms it mentioned, but I certainly have some. Apparently the syndrome has to do with some kind of virus. I don't know about that, but I'm in no doubt whatsoever about my chronic fatigue, and there seem to be similarities between it and the CFS described in the article, especially psychologically, when it comes to the features that distinguish it from ordinary depression (for example, wanting to do things you can't do because of the fatigue that hits you as soon as you start your day, or even as soon as you wake up). Since it was discovered only recently, I have no way of fine-tuning my diagnosis; I'll have to keep treating myself as if I had depression. Yesterday I started taking antidepressants. I haven't noticed anything so far, and nor was I expecting to, since I know they take a few days to have any visible effect. I just want to put an end to this feeling of being crushed, once and for all. Maybe the medication will help, but at the moment it's hard to see a clear future. I can't even catch a glimpse of an acceptable present.

Whatever my illness is, if Alicia's hyperactivity and absences aren't causing it, they must at least be making it worse. Her absences have been getting longer (I mean her absences from our relationship and the way she fills her time completely, without leaving a single gap; not necessarily absences that involve being out of the house). Things are postponed over and over again, and the day when we start "living together" never seems to arrive.

December 9

I'm still waiting to see the effects of the medication: if there have been any so far, they've been entirely negative. I don't feel well at all, and my symptoms and complaints have gotten even worse. I'll see how things progress in the coming days, but I still think circumstances play such an important role that I can expect only so much from unilateral work on myself. It's like being submerged in a pool of poisonous water: if my environment doesn't change, how can I possibly find the formula I need to overcome my condition? I don't know why things are going this way. Maybe there's a basic incompatibility between us that we can't or don't want to see. Whatever it is, time is passing, and far from being resolved or reconciled, things are reaching ever more complicated extremes. The new house, the work that needs to be done on it, and the upcoming move are all making the situation more fraught. And yet everything is subjective: no one's forcing these time frames on us. Alicia is imposing her own rhythm on the preparations for the move, and it's a rhythm I can't keep up with. I still haven't been able to put into practice my system of mentally "placing myself" in the new house and imagining how things will work there. For me this is absolutely crucial, but I don't know if I'll manage it now because everything is in motion, because Alicia has seized control, because the house is taking on forms that haven't been "lived" by me (or anyone else), because this is all being forced upon me—just as here, in this house, rituals and ways of life that I haven't had the chance to examine are imposed on me. We don't do the things we do because of any genuine need; they're not *necessary*. We do them because there's a pattern, an abstract form, acting on us all like a supernatural force.

December 10

I don't know how I expect to have good handwriting in my current state. Never mind, I'm carrying on with these exercises anyway, out of discipline—on the condition that they don't require too much of it. But let me have another go, properly this time. O.K., every now and then it gets better. I'll aim to keep it like this. Good. (How does the G go again?) G G G G G G—no, I'm not convinced at all. G G G. Good, this is the best I can manage today. I feel physically shattered, as if I've been beaten up by half a dozen well-fed soccer hooligans. My mind's in pieces as well, and the days go by without anything getting resolved. I'm tired of formulating survival strategies, wedded to a way of life I have no real incentive to carry on with (almost literally wedded to—a nice unconscious play on words). Everything works asymptotically, like science and reality, two things approaching each other without ever quite meeting. The curve gets closer and closer to the straight line, but no dice.

December 11

I think the antidepressants are starting to do something. I'm definitely noticing the side effects, anyway. As for the primary effects, they might be related to the dreams I had at lunchtime.

I was walking through a building with Dr. NN, and he pointed out a scrawny, dark-skinned, foreign-looking character leaving a room and going down some stairs. The doctor told me this man had been interned there (as a patient or a prisoner) for two (or twenty) years. I remembered this scene later on, because at that moment it had occurred to me to play the lottery, on number two hundred, and afterwards I heard the radio announcing excitedly that that very number had come up. I was amazed, even though I hadn't actually played. I wanted to tell this anecdote to various people on various occasions, but it made the full story too long and complicated, and no one would let me finish; they kept interrupting to talk about other things, and I got frustrated and angry. I was angry at myself, too, for not being able to condense my story, to get to the heart of what I wanted to say. I tried again and again, and every time I ended up going around in circles and getting lost in minor details.

(second sheet)

Another part of the dream took place in a market, while I was looking around for a butcher. I chose a piece of meat, but for some reason I wasn't going to buy it right away and instead tried to hang it back up on a hook that was dangling from the ceiling. Someone from another butcher's stall nearby said he could give me a hand, but I told him I didn't need any help. When I tried to push the meat onto the hook, however, the end of the hook receded into a kind of rag that had been wrapped around its base, so hanging the meat was impossible.

Then someone turned up with a message from a girl who worked in a café in the market, whom I'd apparently asked out on a date. The girl wanted me to know she was waiting until the market closed and she finished her shift. I responded with ridiculous self-importance, sending the messenger back to say it was too late and she'd missed her chance.

At another point in the dream, I'm in the same place as a strange, tall car, maybe a tractor. On the lower part of the vehicle there's a kind of tray for soil and plants, and in it, near the vehicle's large wheels, is a little girl. Her parents were riding in the upper part and couldn't see her very well. I noticed the girl was in danger and thought worriedly: "Her parents don't realize she's big enough to move around now. This way of transporting her would have worked fine when she was much smaller and couldn't go anywhere, but it's not safe anymore."

(third sheet)
There was something like a tree trunk on the ground in the market, and in that tree trunk lived a family (a human family, or a family of fauns—at one point they turn into my friends the X family). Anyway, the family was attached to the tree with some round black rubber straps, which crisscrossed the trunk in whimsical patterns. I drew closer and saw that in among the straps was an extremely dangerous snake, which looked a lot like a strap itself. I tried to separate the (useful) straps from the (dangerous) snake, removing pieces of bark from the tree in the process, but I couldn't finish the job because of the threat from the snake. I was busy with the bark (which at times was a bedsheet and at times something abstract and immaterial) when the snake woke up, and the two of us had a conversation. This conversation included a challenge, and the snake turned into a wolf. I found myself committed to a duel to the death with him, with knives as the weapon, in an adjoining room.

The wolf is wearing clothes. I look at his chest, which is the part I need to aim for, and it's covered by a shirt identical to mine. He lets me go first and bares his breast to my blade. I have various wooden cases piled up on top of one another, all containing various kinds of knives. I choose one and stab the wolf in the heart.

(fourth sheet)

(Reliving it now in my imagination, I see that I aim for the <u>right</u> side of the wolf; it would be <u>my</u> left in the mirror, and this detail seems very significant.)

But I've chosen the wrong knife; its blade folds like paper and the wolf bursts out laughing. I pick another and the same thing happens. I think about a particularly powerful knife I know is in a compartment of one of the cases, but something keeps me from using it. I don't really want to kill anyone; I don't want to feel the metal slicing through flesh, and I don't want to see any blood. The wolf's chest radiates strength and virility. I feel very small and weak, and I'm jealous of that strength and virility I'll never have. In the end, I surrender. I ask the wolf if I can write a letter, saying he can kill me after that. (I have no idea what letter I wanted to write.) The wolf seems satisfied and agrees, but then he's replaced by a woman with round glasses and a sky-blue dress, a woman with some authority there, who tells me the whole thing's absurd and I shouldn't let anyone kill me. The wolf is nowhere to be seen, and I imagine I'm out of danger. I feel relieved but at the same time ashamed of my cowardice, of preferring to be killed than to kill.

December 13

Yesterday I didn't have time to do these exercises, and the day before I didn't so much do exercises as fill page after page with accounts of my dreams. I was pleased to hear that the writing was legible, even though forming the letters couldn't have been further from my mind—unlike now, when I'm concentrating hard on it. Practicing like this is paying off, then. Anyway, yesterday I had another dream. I'll write it down now, and while I do I won't worry about my handwriting.

I was in an enormous bathtub—like a big swimming pool, only narrower and very long—full of soapy water. The soap in the water made it very murky, and because of that nobody could see I was naked. My friend M was with me (and I knew she was also completely naked, though her body was out of sight; only her head was visible above the surface). We were both swimming around happily, and the overriding mood was one of gentle eroticism. But then I notice that the water level in the bathtub is going down; there's much less water than before. I move toward the plug and M is already there, trying to sort it out. "The plug's leaking," she says, struggling to fix it. But her fiddling only loosens it even more, and the water's escaping fast as we try to cover our "modesty" with our hands and arms, twisting our bodies so as little as possible is on display. The gentle eroticism disappears and is replaced by a certain anxiety about what's happening, but at the same time we find the situation funny and start laughing. There are other women outside the bathtub, and we ask them to bring something to cover us up. The bathtub is in the middle of the countryside.

December 14

Last night I had another dream about water. This one took place in a little cove in the river or the sea. To the right there was a wooden bridge, or jetty, that extended a certain distance over the water. There were also a few pieces of wood in view, some floating and some poking out above the surface like concrete piles. I often used to swim there, always for long stretches of time, and I was feeling happy, even though Stalin had just come to power and there was a bit of political tension in the air. The public still didn't see him as a malevolent figure, but I knew no good would come of him. Nevertheless, I didn't feel personally afraid—it was as if I had a kind of immunity. I even advised other people, who looked like tourists (and maybe I was a tourist too), to try to get out of that country, though I carried on swimming peacefully myself.

In other news (and now it's time to pay attention to my calligraphical duties again—though if "calli-graphy" means "beautiful writing," maybe graphical duties are enough for me), today was the first Friday of the new phase of my relationship with Alicia. We've agreed that Fridays will be days dedicated entirely to us, to our communication and intimacy. In fact, this "day" was reduced to about an hour, as I predicted. Alicia says it's something new to get used to and she still needs to adjust a few details (or, in her words, "grease the wheels a bit"; I think it'll take a lot of grease). And so the situation remains the same: the circumstantial always displacing the essential; our existences endlessly revolving around stupid, pointless things; and life passing us by for other people to live, if they want to. Time to take my antidepressants.

December 15

And so it goes. I don't know what else I can say. So it goes. (The title of a novel by Saul Bellow comes to mind: *Dangling Man.* I'm also dangling, in a way, not dangling in the sense of my feet not touching the floor, but in the sense of a dangling participle. A pause, uncertainty, reaching the end of one word without finding the right one to follow. You could also say "Man in Brackets," though it would be more accurate to say that I'm a man located after the first bracket, wondering where the second one is. A temporary emergency phase, but one that's extended and extended and never properly defined. It's like going to a hotel for two or three days and then staying for months, years, living out of a suitcase or bag the whole time and not sorting anything out "until I'm settled somewhere.")

This situation appears to be caused by the clash of two wills, Alicia's and mine. If I were alone, the parenthesis would have been much shorter. But I have to wait for her, though waiting seems completely nonsensical by now because I know she's never going to arrive. Maybe I do it out of curiosity, wanting to see what new tricks she comes up with, but whatever my reasons, I have no excuse for this interminable postponement of my own self, except laziness, except stupidity, except negligence (a word derived from a Latin verb meaning "to look at with indifference") (and in-difference is the inability to differentiate; it refers to a scale of values that isn't really there). (And so I look at myself indifferently, ascribing no value to anything within me, devalued in my own eyes.) How can I get out of this situation? I hope graphology can help me, since I've been forsaken by the gods.

The Discourse

December 15

Today the topic of the dog has been thrust upon me once more—because the dog has disappeared. At least, he'd disappeared as of last night, and if this morning he came back and then went out again, I know nothing about it because I slept until past noon. Anyway, I can't help worrying about him, and his absence is impossible to ignore. Although it's been over a year since he widened the gap in the fence and learned his way around the streets, a disappearance like this is unusual. He's stayed out late before and not come back until after dark, but I don't think he's ever gone missing so decisively. What's more, since moving day is getting closer and we don't know if there'll be room for the dog in the new house, we've been starting to think about what we might do with him. For example, we could give him to someone who lives farther out than us, ideally in the countryside, and can find some space for him. This matter has already caused some conflict, since the dog is very much part of the family and sending him away would be hard for everyone—for the dog and for us, I mean. But his disappearance now doesn't solve the problem; it just makes us feel all the more guilty.

The day he widened the gap by himself and went through it to the empty lot next door, he returned a few minutes later as if wanting to ensure that it worked properly in both directions. Then he went straight back out and explored every square inch of the lot with olfactory relish, rolling around in the long grass and urinating at a number of strategic points to mark his territory. That day, he went through the gap over and over again in both directions. On the following day, he left the empty lot and went out onto the pavement. A few days later he was crossing the street, at first without looking and at great risk to himself, though later he learned to check for cars. Now he's an expert, but accidents can happen to anyone, especially someone like the dog, who's so much governed by his instincts. We have a child in this house, too—Ignacio—and he's often risked life and limb careening across the street without looking, worried about the fate of a ball that's slipped from his hands or bounced the wrong way off the wall and ended up in the road. The instinct to run after the ball overrules all the awareness of danger we've instilled in him.

The risk is far greater in the dog's case, since his instincts are stronger and his awareness, if we can call it that, is much weaker. Especially when he's in heat, and his aggression is running high. Yesterday, for example, he had an altercation with a little dog on a leash that was trotting past with its owner. He doesn't normally go in for scenes like that. I heard the commotion and went out to get him, and when I made him go into the house he carried on growling for a long time afterwards, as if his rage would never subside.

We need to be careful around him when he's like this, too, though he's never bitten anyone seriously. If he thinks we're attacking him or invading his personal space, he'll immediately retaliate with growls or a violent bark and a snap at the air. Once he actually bit my shoes, as if even at the height of his atavistic passions, he'd felt somehow protective toward his owners and directed his fury somewhere he knew it wouldn't do any harm.

I'm monumentally bored of talking about the dog. I feel as if my discourse has denatured completely, as if it's lost its original form and rhythm and I'm now writing automatically, out of habit. But I haven't forgotten what I'm trying to achieve, and I'm wondering if this boredom might be a necessary prelude to a surprise attack, the sudden capture of the discourse's real content, which I'm still waiting to find. I don't know. Or maybe, if I want to carry on writing, I should stop for a bit and wait for inspiration to strike.

*

Unlike what seems to happen with humans, being in heat sharpens the dog's wits. For months, he refused with incredible stubbornness to learn, even by trial and error, that if he came into the house he'd be sent straight out to the courtyard, where his kennel is now, in disgrace. We've been doing this a few times a day for a very long time, and yet he's only recently caught on.

He discovered he could get into the house the day after he learned how to use the gap in the fence, and what a discovery it was: finally he understood the relationship between the front and the back ends of the house, which it seems he'd previously thought were completely unconnected. Ever since then, it's been his life's ambition to get into the house and live with us inside it. There are a number of reasons why we can't allow this, among them his habit of urinating in corners and on the legs of the furniture—no one house-trained him when he was young and it seems impossible to do it now. He's also overly exuberant when welcoming visitors, and his impassioned displays of affection can get somewhat out of hand. With a few exceptions, he's far too positive about everyone.

Anyway, when he discovered he could get out of the back garden through the gap in the fence, cross the whole of the empty lot and run a few yards down the pavement, then come into the house through the front door, a whole world of possibilities opened up to him. I had to make a kind of miniature door out of an old iron grate and some wires, which I used to close off the gap in the fence whenever we thought it was a bad time to have the dog hanging around near the front door, waiting for his chance to slip inside. For a few months, then, we were able to regulate the flow of the dog around the house at our convenience. It was all going very well, albeit not entirely effortlessly, until one day the dog was in heat and learned—don't ask me how—to remove the grate. We tried a few techniques for reinforcing it, only for him to realize he could escape around the other side through a few badly filled holes in the hedge. At first I managed to cover one of these holes with a sheet of metal borrowed from a neighbor, but then the dog made another. That one was too difficult to close off, because of the size of the metal sheet it would need and the fact that it was surrounded by a profusion of shrubs and other vegetation, which complicate all human endeavors. And that was how we lost control of the dog until, the heat gone (from him or from the female dog who got him riled up), he seemed to forget about this particular modus operandi. But now he's remembered, and once again we've lost control.

It was in the middle of the saga of the dog's comings and goings that the cat appeared. A very beautiful white cat, with yellow-green eyes and a particularly haughty sort of elegance. The first time I saw him, he was in the empty lot next door, and I'd just moved the sheet of metal aside to let the dog out. I thought things were really going to kick off. And the dog did indeed make a move in the cat's direction, but the cat didn't seem to care. He looked straight at the dog, seeming to hold him back with his gaze, then turned and stalked off, calmly and gracefully, and for reasons beyond my comprehension, the dog didn't move an inch. He simply stood and watched the cat vacate the lot through one of the broken gates and emerge onto the pavement. The cat hadn't run away, which would have led to a chase; he'd merely turned his back on the dog and departed peacefully, his gait slow and nonchalant, his head held high and his tail aloft. At that moment, all the dog did was cautiously sniff the places the cat had been and the routes he'd walked, like a police officer collecting fingerprints in order to capture the criminal at a later date.

Exercises

December 16

It's hard not to be frightened when you realize you can't rely very much on yourself. I've played all my cards and lost, and now there are no more chances. Repeat my Buenos Aires adventure? Things aren't so easy now (not that they were ever very easy), because the circumstances have changed and I have that first experience weighing on me. It was a good thing to do once, but it would be a terrible thing to repeat. Montevideo? Aside from the weather, there's nothing appealing about that. And who knows what I'd do to pay the bills.

A couple of days ago I made a dangerous move, though now I'm glad I did: I sent a fax to the agency that buys crosswords from me, requesting a new rate. If it works out, the extra money might shake things up a bit. If it doesn't work out . . . well, I'll have to think of something else.

Really, the most difficult part of all this is making the drastic decision to separate from Alicia. If I could do it, cleanly and irreversibly, I know I'd immediately find a way to move forward. But I haven't been able to make the decision. I speculate about it, but something very powerful—more powerful than fear—is still holding me back. I need to explore this more deeply. But I'm afraid of deceiving myself, or allowing her to deceive me. Everything can seem so clear, and then she makes another move, plays another trick, and suddenly it's all muddled up again and shining with the lights of (false) hope. And so I decide to go on hoping, and every new hope exhausts me a little more, sucks a little more life from me, and dismantles my remaining self-esteem, until the only thing I have left is the pointless lucidity with which I passively observe the way I'm going under once and for all.

December 17

I think I've worked out why these exercises, which were meant to be about handwriting, are always so quick to deteriorate into other things. According to my theory, it's because I have no direct communication with Alicia. When I started these exercises, I used to leave the pages on the nightstand so she could monitor my progress, or lack thereof, and as a result they naturally became a way of telling her things—hence the anxiety that makes me write too fast when I have something important to say. It's a strange existence, to say the least, always living, and thinking, in relation to somebody else. Most of the time that person isn't even there, and you don't know when they'll be back. So you go on writing, page after page, at first genuinely trying to focus on the handwriting, but all too often turning into a kind of shipwrecked sailor stuffing messages into bottles and sending them out to sea. In this case there's no doubt about whether the messages will arrive, but the bottle image seems fitting nevertheless—as does the image of the exile, which is what I've been feeling like for a while now, even more so in Colonia than in Buenos Aires. Anyway, the point is to fill these pages with lines of script, trying to be patient and forming the letters with care.

December 24

Now, after a run of difficult days, I'm making another attempt to connect with myself through these exercises. It's hopeless, of course, because "tonight is Christmas Eve and tomorrow is Christmas Day," as the tango goes (and I can almost hear Gardel's voice as I write). This means an onslaught of social engagements, intrusions, intolerable noise, and unhealthy food that's completely unsuited to the time of year. Until now I've always successfully avoided the whole thing; most of the time I arrange to be by myself, reading a detective novel or doing some writing, occasionally seeing a friend (often someone Jewish) so we can get through the dark days together, eating reasonably and having reasonable conversations. But I'm not currently the "artist of my own destiny," as the old self-help manuals used to say we should be, and instead I'm bound by the omnipotent will of a woman who is in turn completely bound by social conventions, an activist fighting for the cause of wakefulness, a solar woman (and I'm a lunar man). I wonder how much longer I'll put up with this way of "life," in which the essential, profound, true, authentic questions—for which we were created—are consistently displaced, indefinitely postponed, forgotten and sometimes even abused. I wonder how much longer I'll keep up this cycle of hoping and losing hope. At my age I don't have the luxury of waiting very long, and already too much time has passed since I was last in touch with myself. Happy Holidays.

December 27

I need to look into the idea of independence more deeply. It could, depending on how things go, either support a separation from Alicia or strengthen the relationship. If nothing else, it will be a break in the current status quo, which is the source of all my pathologies. On the subject of independence, this morning (or indeed around noon) the Unconscious presented me with quite a slipup. I was in my usual confused state upon getting out of bed, so I won't be able to dredge up the full chain of my thoughts, but I remember one of its links relating to someone I knew. At that moment, to my immense surprise, I thought something like: "But Alicia doesn't know that person," even though she knows them perfectly well. I realized then that my image of Alicia, or rather my internal perception of Alicia, has been replaced with that of my mother. This pernicious identification of Alicia with my mother has been going on for some time (in dreams, for example), and I've never paid it enough attention——especially considering how much it surely bothers me. But what happened this morning made me confront it, and I was able to do so willingly. I was also able to acknowledge that this idea has been trying to attract my attention for a while now, but that I've been ignoring it, refusing to think about it, brushing it to one side of my consciousness. It must be the main disrupting factor in my relationship with Alicia. I need to stay alert and consider the matter more carefully.

The Discourse

December 30

A lot of things have happened over the past two weeks. Too many for someone who'd rather turn inward for a while, detached from pressing obligations; someone who wants to let the inner discourse become clearer, and allow themselves to pay it sufficient attention. But today I've had a tune stuck in my head instead of the discourse, and for me that's a clear sign I haven't slept well. Not only last night, but for many nights now. And for various reasons.

The story of the dog at one point took a tragic turn. He already had a habit, during what I call his time in heat—when, as I've said, he becomes manic and aggressive—of disappearing from home for long stretches of time, sometimes even overnight. There was a period of a few days in which he passed only fleetingly through the house each afternoon to wolf down a few pieces of meat. And then one morning, around midday on Wednesday the seventeenth, if I remember correctly, the maid gave me the bad news as soon as I was awake: the dog had turned up injured, looking like he had "something in his eye," and now he was out in the courtyard. It was a moving sight. The dog was hunched in a corner in the shadows, his head bowed, and every fiber of his being seemed to say he was depressed—and in pain too, no doubt. I had to knock hard on the window before he eventually, laboriously, lifted his head and met my gaze. It wasn't a face I wanted to see again in a hurry. His right eye socket looked completely empty.

I was convinced he'd lost an eye, and the vet later confirmed this diagnosis. By then I was feeling very uncomfortable indeed. I immediately remembered all this written testimony about the dog and his freedom. I remembered how I'd been largely responsible for said freedom and how when the dog eventually decided to widen the gap between the metal post and the wall, it was because I'd tempted him into it. This freedom, I thought, had cost him dearly. And however much I told myself it was better this way, that a life without freedom is worthless, etc., there was no ignoring the guilt eating away at my insides. Maybe that's why—though there were practical reasons as well—I stopped writing this. I'd already noticed, a few years before, that this kind of writing has uncontrollable magical effects, and I can't escape a powerful, superstitious feeling of awe and trepidation whenever I do it, as if I were stealing fire from the gods.

There are other kinds of writing, let's call them literary, which have never had this "magical" power for me. What I refer to as my inspired writing, for example, was something I did compulsively; it came ready-made from the inner depths. But when I try to address what people call reality, when my writing becomes current and biographical, I can't help unconsciously bringing these mysterious hidden mechanisms into motion. Then they begin to interact secretly, or so it seems, with various visible effects.

*

Now, believe it or not, the dog is cured. If you look at him a certain way you still sometimes notice his right eye drifting a little, but despite a small white mark like a scar on its surface, we know he can see through it. For a few days he kept it more and more tightly shut, then he began to open it, though all you could see of the eye itself was bloodshot and crooked. For several days after that, the dog was the spitting image of Sartre: his whole right eye was visible and no longer bloodshot, but it had a tendency to roll in unexpected directions. Now the dog is almost entirely himself again, fit and full of self-confidence.

I, on the other hand, have been tossing and turning the past few nights with some highly erotic dreams that leave me exhausted. My almost constant eczema and liver trouble aren't helping, either. I've come to believe—and it's frustrating to be stuck in such a superstitious line of thinking—that these dreams reveal a kind of curse. Erotic dreams themselves don't bother me (in fact, I love them), but what definitely does bother me is some of the women chosen to feature in them with me. I don't want to go into detail, but I was struck by how in the first dream, with a contemptible and unpleasant woman, I orgasmed fully—although in my physical reality this wasn't matched by an actual release of semen—and the following night another similar woman took part in what wasn't exactly an erotic dream, but a recurring erotic fantasy. I was in a semiconscious state, a kind of hypnotic trance. The scene was repeated a few times, and I kept drifting in and out of consciousness, but it was as if I was awake the whole time and yet unable to escape from the fantasy. And when I woke up the next day, I felt exhausted and lethargic again. Last night, which was the third night, I don't remember dreaming about anything in particular, but I still didn't sleep well. Today I have the same old tune in my head, and it's pushed out the discourse in all its forms.

Meanwhile, in my waking hours, the countdown to moving day is picking up speed. The workers are finishing off the last urgent, essential jobs in the new house (after which there'll be more jobs, and more still, for a very long time), and the thought of putting things in boxes, emptying out the furniture, and then distributing our furniture and things throughout the new house in a completely different arrangement is quite overwhelming. And in the middle of all this, we have the "holidays."

*

The agency didn't refuse my request to be paid more for my crosswords. Instead, they said they no longer required my services. According to their fax, they looked at the numbers and realized it wasn't working out for them, even at the normal rate. So I am unemployed. I don't know what worries me more, the fact of not having a job or the way people around here have started looking at me. Somehow or other, through a comment here, a gesture there, they make me feel like I've done something wrong. Like I've become *suspicious*.

December 31

I have a sneaking suspicion that the cat was to blame for the dog nearly losing an eye. After that initial sighting in the empty lot next door, I spotted the cat again a few days later, when by some strange twist of fate I'd woken up very early. I first noticed him from the bedroom window: he was at the far end of the garden, a little white smudge among the plants by the hedge. I looked more closely and saw it was him, and was surprised that he'd ventured onto the dog's turf. When I let the dog out, the cat, instead of running away, left at a leisurely pace through a small gap between some sheets of metal and the ground. With time, the cat grew bolder, and his appearances became more regular. One day Alicia came across him, and being a cat lover she wasted no time in offering him some milk in a little cup with no handle. The cat came over and lapped it up.

As he became more sure of himself, he started making demands: a cup of milk was no longer enough, and he used to sit under the kitchen window or by the wooden door with the mosquito panels, meowing and meowing. The dog put up with the cat's presence for the most part, even showing him a certain cautious respect, but the trouble began when the dog realized the cat was also being fed meat. At mealtimes, the dog would find the courage to charge at the cat, chasing him away and stealing his food. I soon learned to feed them separately, the cat in the back garden and the dog in the courtyard, where his kennel is and where he spends the night. But later, when he was back outside, the dog would sniff his way frenziedly, obsessively around the places where the cat had been eating, bustling along like a jealous detective and seeming almost enraged by the whole business.

The dog then took to picking his food up in his mouth and carrying it to the empty lot next door, ostensibly so he could eat in peace. This had me fooled until I realized that sometimes he'd then abandon his food and go and hide in the long grass, keeping watch through the wire fence to see whether I was feeding the cat. If I was, he'd come crashing through the hole in the fence like an omen and tear toward the cat at a furious gallop.

Around the same time, the dog took to greeting me effusively whenever I went into the back garden. Over he'd come, wagging his tail, looking at me adoringly and resting his paws on my legs so I could stroke his head. As soon as I'd given him a rub between the ears and a few pats on the back, the dog would turn his head, narrow his eyes, and glare straight at the cat in arrogant disdain. He hadn't really wanted affection: the whole thing was a performance put on for the benefit of the cat, to show him that he, the dog, was the favorite.

At that point in the cat's life with us, he was, in our eyes, a she. And not only was he a she, but he was also expecting kittens. During the cat's first days in the back garden, Alicia—a doctor, and apparently also a cat expert—went out and examined the animal carefully, returning with a decisive verdict: this is a female cat, and she's pregnant. I thought anxiously about how many cats we'd end up with after a year or two and tried to work out what we'd spend on pet food; by then, feeding both the cat and the dog involved quite an expense. And I wasn't keen on the idea of a whole troupe of kittens meowing under the kitchen window, either, making their demands in the particularly insistent way cats do. Admittedly, when the cat awoke from one of her innumerable siestas in the sun, stretched, and strolled airily off, her tail waving high, I did see two small, perfectly round shapes poking out quite clearly between her hind legs, under the rectum. Since I steer clear of all medical and feline matters in this house, however, for a long time I respected Alicia's verdict and went on treating the pregnant cat with all the respect owing to her in her condition as a female and an expectant mother. I let her come and rub herself voluptuously against my legs, and I even started applying a curative lotion to her head and eyes for a rash I'd seen she had. Then Alicia also noticed the existence of the balls, and the cat's gender was no longer in doubt.

So things went on, the only difference being the dog's worsening moods and increasingly erratic behavior, which could reasonably be attributed to his being in heat. He spent more time than ever methodically escaping from the back garden in order to sneak into the house through the front door. He also learned to open the wooden door with the mosquito panels on it, when it was so swollen with damp it couldn't be bolted shut, and used that as another way in. All the dog wanted was to get inside the house and thereby show his dominance over the cat. Since we wouldn't let him, he instead waited by the front door and greeted anyone who arrived with a practical demonstration of the overpowering joy their visit brought him. For me, these few months were a period of intensive work, what with feeding the two animals, separating them at mealtimes, rubbing lotion onto the cat, making a fuss of the dog to build up his self-esteem, moving the dog from the courtyard to the back garden, and sending him back to the courtyard in disgrace when he snuck in through the front door. All in all, this took up a large part of my day, and my energies.

It's not that I didn't have more important things to do—such as my work, which now included writing articles for the newspaper—but I was held captive by an ecosystem.

Then various things happened that, after they'd taken place a few times, changed my opinion of the cat and made me treat him differently. I began to notice the dog looking scared to push open the door to the back garden, which he used to do vigorously whenever he pleased, or whenever we sent him outside. Now he'd make a timid attempt, barely nudging the door, as if too weak to do anything else, and then stop and look up at me plaintively. I realized the cat was often on the other side, apparently waiting for his chance to attack.

One afternoon when I was petting the cat, he rolled onto his back for the first time and started playing the way cats like to, trapping my hand between his front paws. But then he got up, rubbed himself against my legs a few times, walked around behind me, and gave me a scratch and a sharp nip on the calf. I didn't like this one bit, and what I liked even less was the way he walked off in supercilious triumph, waving his tail from side to side. Exactly the same thing happened a few days later, and this time his claws went deeper and drew a few drops of blood. I had to put iodine on the wound. And so I resolved to stop playing with that treacherous cat, and these days I eye him with suspicion.

Another time, I saw him waiting patiently by the gap in the fence the dog uses to come back from the empty lot, as if guarding the entrance to a mousehole. When I happened to glance over later, he was in the same place, and the dog was making his way through the gap. I saw with my own eyes how the cat swiped at him with his claws, and I heard the dog's howl of pain. That was it for the cat, as far as I was concerned. I stopped feeding him, and when he became particularly tiresome, meowing endlessly under the kitchen window, I chased him away with jugfuls of water, or even the hose. I focused on restoring the dog's confidence in himself and in my affection for him. I tried to make him see that things were different now; I started feeding him in the back garden, for example, and leaving the cat to meow outside the window or the door in vain.

Before all this, the cat had carried out a cautious, systematic, and highly meticulous investigation of the inside of our house. One day I came across him standing at the kitchen door, not asking for any food, and I left the door ajar as if to invite him in. He took a few steps over the threshold but then raced straight back out again as if he'd seen a ghost. The same thing happened a few days later, but this time it was clear he had a plan: as soon as he was inside, he made a beeline for the bedroom. He explored it systematically, inch by inch, including the dark corners behind the wardrobe; he peered around the back of the bedside tables and inspected the space under the bed. He examined everything with a computer-like intelligence, compiling and storing the data. After that, he slowly progressed into the back garden. His research continued over the next few days. First he retraced his steps through the bedroom, only more briskly this time, as if to confirm certain details he already knew, and then he began venturing a little farther into the house every day: the kitchen, the dining room, the front hall . . .

That was how trusted this perfidious animal had become by the time I uncovered his perfidy and put an end to his food and kind treatment.

Exercises

January 2, 1991

I'm still suffering from various illnesses, or from one illness that's showing itself in various ways—in particular, through some persistent eczema that's sticking around for longer than it usually does. I'm also having digestive trouble, most likely related to my liver. There must be something psychological behind all this. Today I had a dream it seemed important to retain, but not long after waking up I'd forgotten what it was. A curtain's been set up in my mind, a blockade in the form of an obsessive melody, and the more I try to remember the dream, the louder and faster the music becomes. This obstruction seems like a maneuver on the part of what Freud calls the *superego*, since it's the consciousness that's struggling to remember the dream and the *id* must be what produced it. Why this repression? Why is something it tried to do and, to some extent, achieved (becoming conscious) then rudely pushed under once again? (Come to think of it, I wonder if it has to do with the fact that I've learned to interpret my dreams; the superego now *knows* about this skill of mine, and although it begrudgingly allows its contents to be seen in dreams by means of symbols, it doesn't want me to remember those symbols afterwards because it knows I may well be able to decipher them.) (But, again, what possible interest can the superego have in keeping the ego in the dark?) I'm not entirely convinced by that explanation, I have to admit. There must be more to it. Perhaps my conscious self has something to do with the repressive maneuvers after all. It could be that the self feels overloaded with responsibilities coming from the outside world, and so *I myself* don't feel like taking care of things in the inner world, which is certainly what happens, for example, when it comes to literature. Every time I feel the urge to write a story or a novel, I repress it, thinking: "If I make a start on this, who knows if I'll be allowed to finish it. I'll be interrupted and the beautiful impulse will be left incomplete, frustrated, and ruined."

The Discourse

January 2

If I'm still writing so patiently and in so much detail about these essentially very mundane things, it's probably out of inertia: the abstract discourse is still AWOL for now, and the music's still there in its place, sometimes louder and more insistent, sometimes so soft and subtle I'm barely aware of it. The tune seems to come from a kind of mechanism for erasing dreams. I fear it all traces back to a divided self: on one side, the me who wants to recover the dream, and on the other, the me who doesn't want to hand it over. The first, inquisitive me is my old self, the one I've known all my life and who got used to recording dreams, savoring them, writing about them, and even trying to interpret them. I have countless pieces of paper with dreams from different periods of my life written down on them. But now there's a new me (much more influenced by the superego, yes, but me at the end of the day) that's more focused on external, practical matters (which I've called "mundane," maybe unfairly but definitely angrily). This new self has seized possession of my being, it's taken root decisively in my life, and all without me accepting it (and when I say "me" now, I'm talking about the old me). It has too much control and there's no getting rid of it, and I've yet to find a way of reconciling both selves into a single unique and powerful self. It all seems to come back to the problem of time—whether the lack of it, or the inability to situate both selves harmoniously within it.

I've just remembered a dream I was in fact able to retain, at least partially, and perhaps this dream expresses the problem I'm talking about. I've forgotten large swathes of the plot, but I can remember some of the ending.

In the bit I can remember, I was walking down the street with a man who seemed very friendly, agreeable, and somehow protective. I felt comfortable with him. And yet he was a policeman who appeared to have caught me, and he was taking me to the station to fill out a form. The purpose of the form wasn't clear, and I was afraid that once we got to the police station they'd arrest me or lock me up and I'd have to stay there for a very long time. The agreeable policeman advised me to introduce myself calmly to the people in the police station, hiding the fact that I had any reason to be concerned or defensive. He pointed me toward a door and said he'd wait outside; for some reason, he couldn't go in himself. His mission ended there. So I went in alone, edging through a narrow gap with the wall to my left and a pool table to my right. There were also a few people there playing pool. At the far end of the large room I found myself in was a booth with a little window on one side, covered by vertical bars. I approached it nervously, but when I got closer I realized there was no one inside it and I'd have to wait patiently to be attended to. At that moment, I woke up.

I feel like I'm going round in circles. If I'm not mistaken, these pages began with me talking about almost exactly the same thing, namely the inability of my consciousness to take charge of certain unconscious contents that are struggling to surface. I definitely need help—someone who, just like in the dream, will lead me obligingly toward the ordeal of the prison cell or the complicated form, to a place where I'll somehow be judged or critically examined. Unfortunately, there are no therapists in this town who could help me. The only suitable person (apart from Alicia, who should be ruled out for obvious reasons) is someone I know well enough to invalidate any therapeutic ties. I've thought about healers, and people have suggested homeopathy. I'm happy to give anything a go. But what I really need is a psychotherapist, and there aren't any nearby, and for various reasons I'm stuck here and can't easily travel.

On top of all this, there's the imminent move to the new house. The house we're selling is metaphorically falling to pieces (and physically, too, I could almost add). When you know you have to leave a place, never to return, it's impossible to go on living there comfortably. You stop being where you are, so to speak, and instead spend your time projecting yourself more and more forcefully into the place where you'll soon be living. If I look at my books it's to think about tying them into tidy little packages, and that's how it goes with everything. If something is lost or broken, it no longer gets replaced. If some furniture's in the wrong position, it no longer gets put back. We're living here temporarily, as if in a hotel, constantly counting and recounting the number of days and hours left before we move. The effort that moving will involve, however, has yet to fully sink in. I find it impossible to imagine moving day, when I'll get out of bed in this house and then go to sleep in the same bed in a different house; in between the two there's exertion, complications, work I don't think I can face.

The thing is, I've accumulated too many moves lately. After more than thirty-five years in the same building, over the past six years I've moved three times, and this will be the fourth—and that's not even counting all the stays in hotels and the houses of friends and relatives, or the month in a little house here in Colonia. It's a lot of change for a man who generally gets extremely attached to places.

Exercises

January 3

It's been pointed out to me, entirely fairly, that these exercises have lost all their calligraphical intent. My writing is now intelligible, though, so in a sense they're still doing their job. Consequently, as I write this I'm trying to pay as much attention as I can to forming the letters. I shall devote today's exercises to developing patience in my writing, focusing on the shapes I'm forming and not on what I'm trying to say. At this juncture, however, I'm going to risk something very difficult: I'm going to attempt to write about a dream I had recently without losing sight of my calligraphical duties.

Just before waking up, I had the third in a series of erotic dreams. The dreams in the series all have similar characteristics, and ever since the first one, I've had a sense of being subject to the machinations of witchcraft. The second dream, unlike the first, contained not a complete sexual act, but an erotic scene that was repeated over and over throughout the night, while I was half-asleep, or half-awake, or in a kind of hypnotic trance. Today's dream seemed like a continuation of the series, which is becoming subtler as it goes along. You could even say that today's was a normal dream, and certainly nothing about it suggested spells or curses. However, it must belong to the series because, like the other dreams, it features downtrodden women. The woman in the second dream was attractive in many ways, but repellent in many others. And today's was the same, though she would have been attractive a few years ago and you could have a great intellectual exchange with her. I think the series—witchcraft aside—shows a process taking place that relates to the <u>anima</u>

(see Jung), and as it goes on I find myself feeling a little better, physically and spiritually.

January 6

The Three Kings brought me diddly-squat. I'll have to do things myself from now on. (There's a profound truth behind these lighthearted words.)

Last night I had another dream in what's now undeniably a series: a series of dreams about groups of people I don't know. I had the first one in Buenos Aires, and the others, two or three of them, here in Colonia. I think they all relate (among other things, of course) to my real-life existence among strangers, as if in exile.

The dream was about a journey. We were getting ready to set off from somewhere, and I was introduced to a young woman I didn't know, whose name was Cristina. Then, along with some other people, we were driven away in a horse-drawn carriage. Of all the people traveling with me (at least seven or eight in total), the only one I knew was Jorge, who's some kind of professional and a friend of Alicia's. He seemed to be joining us as a special guest. From that point on I had a secondary role in the dream, as if I were part of the scenery. Everyone else seemed to be acting with a particular purpose in mind, but I didn't know what it was.

(second page)

I stayed in the background, asking no questions, going with the flow, and looking after Cristina, who at times seemed very young, almost a child.

The group organized itself the way groups of men by themselves usually do: united by their common purpose, whatever it was, the men talked among themselves and ignored the women, who later, when we reached our destination, seemed like little more than servants. I acted as the link between the group of men and, by means of Cristina, the group of women.

Eventually we arrived at the gates of a country residence or farmhouse, and the owner met us at the door. He was an old man with the definite look of a local big shot, tyrant, or mafia boss. During the journey, the city of Colonia had been specifically discussed.

In the street, a few women were setting up long tables for a banquet in the evening light. We went into the house, which was big, old, and complicated to navigate. I soon lost sight of the group of men. And of Cristina. I walked around some more, and at last I found the men in a room that looked like a radio station or recording studio. They were all behind the glass making a news bulletin about Jorge, who seemed to be the "star" of the gathering. Cristina turned up outside the room and knocked very loudly on the glass of the outer door. I signaled to her not to make any noise because of the recording and then left, and the two of us went for a walk.

The Discourse

January 6

There are some pointless things the soul can't do without. I could go further: it's *only* pointless things that the soul can't do without (though not *all* pointless things). But I won't go that far, because I don't want to make an extreme claim that I'll later regret. These extreme claims are the product of my circumstances, of my rebellion against my circumstances. Since my life is shaped by ideas of what's functional, I become too impassioned in my defense of pointless things. I lose my sense of balance and good judgment.

These reflections of mine must have been prompted by the fact that I'm home alone again (and it's a Sunday). I love these weekends when I can be by myself, though I deplore how short-lived my solitude always is. It's not that I'd like to live alone; what I really want is to live among people who respect my solitude and need for silence and digressions. Alicia is learning to do this, but it's not enough; I wish she could accept this world *ideologically,* as it were, and eventually come to enjoy peace and silence the way I do.

When I woke up by myself in the house this morning, surrounded by immense silence, immense peace, I found myself thinking about a whole assortment of pointless things—the sort the soul appreciates. Over breakfast, I read a few of Dylan Thomas's letters. In one of them, written when he was a young man, he said that nothing ephemeral could ever be beautiful to him, that beauty is about eternity. I disagreed, since I can't think of anything that isn't ephemeral. Even pure forms need an ephemeral mind in order to exist. Beauty is in the mind, not in things, and pure forms exist only in the mind.

Then I put on a cassette I'd chosen at random and the first thing I heard was a cover, by a group I didn't know, of a song made popular a long time ago by Enrique Rodríguez's tango orchestra (something like "Hungarian Nights" or "Love in Istanbul"). Listening to it felt wonderful, and I immediately recalled the image of a large warehouse or depot Alicia and I had seen a few days ago on a little beach by the racecourse; an old building covered in panes of glass. Looking at it, I'd wished I had a camera with me to capture that glass landscape (unbroken in some places, but cracked in many more) in the particular light of the sunset. And as well as the glass, there were pieces of disused machinery and metal coils in the fields, among the weeds. Wonderful: I derive an almost erotic pleasure from contemplating certain ruins—empty houses, demolished houses—especially when they're overgrown with vegetation.

I remember a house I saw on Cerro Pan de Azúcar. It was abandoned or incomplete, almost the skeleton of a house; perhaps it had been abandoned before it was finished. There was a tree growing inside it, and one of its branches had wound its way through a window. Dylan Thomas can say what he likes; this is my idea of beauty. As, too, was a disused church I saw on the same road, which leads from Piriapolis to Pan de Azúcar. Contemplating it, I think, constituted my first genuine mystical-religious experience. The building was completely falling down, and there was a hideous wooden crucifix over the entrance (I was later told that this crucifix had turned up on the coast nearby, carried there by the waves).

Enrique Rodríguez's orchestra is somewhat similar to all this. Once, when Alicia and I were driving home after a long trip, for much of the journey there was a program about Enrique Rodríguez on the radio. It was extraordinary, marred only by the fact that I couldn't share it with Alicia—she was at the wheel, concentrating hard, and most unimpressed at having to listen to such a racket.

I can enjoy Bach and Vivaldi as much as she does, and I can tell the difference between Bach or Vivaldi and Enrique Rodríguez. But just then it seemed impossible to explain to her how that orchestra, for me, was like contemplating a ruin overgrown with vegetation. Not because the orchestra was around so long ago, though in a way that heightens the effect, but because, even at the time, Enrique Rodríguez's original intention was always a ruin overgrown with vegetation. That's what his music tells me, and it's what, after breakfast today, was woven into my secret argument with Dylan Thomas and my memory of the sunset on the beach by the racecourse. And that's how I recovered an essential part of myself, which I'd lost in the chaos of recent years.

*

People think, almost unanimously, that what interests me is writing. But what really interests me is remembering. In some languages, the word "remember" comes from the old word for awaken, and that's how I like to think of it. I forget whether it relates to the word for heart as well, but I hope it does. After all, remembering things sometimes means knowing them by heart.

Often people even say: "There's a plot for one of your novels," as if I went around in search of plots for novels and not in search of myself. If I write it's in order to remember, to awaken my sleeping soul, to stir up my mind and discover its secret pathways. Most of my stories are fragments of my soul's memory, not inventions.

The soul has its own way of seeing things. It contains elements of our waking lives, but also elements that are particular and personal to it; the soul is part of a higher order of universal understanding that our consciousness can't access directly. The soul's conception of what happens in and around us, then, is much more complete than anything the narrow, limited self could ever perceive.

Today all those different kinds of ruins came back to me, and I knew it was my soul's way of saying, "I am those ruins."

My semi-erotic contemplation of the ruins is really a narcissistic contemplation of myself. And although it comes at a price, and despite the sadness of what's being contemplated, it feels good. When I look at myself in the mirror and see someone I don't like, I think: at least it's someone I can trust. The same thing happens with this inner contemplation. It doesn't matter if I'm looking at an ugly picture as long as it's authentic.

Of course, I don't know to what extent my soul is really mine. It's more that I belong to this soul, which is not, as more than one philosopher has said, necessarily even inside me. It's simply something I don't know about, and the *self* is only a part—shaped by a certain practical awareness—of a vast ocean that transcends me and in no way belongs to me, a specimen that has emerged, or is emerging, from an immense sea of nucleic acid. But what's behind it, and what impulse is expressing itself by means of the acid? That desire, that curiosity, that greed latent in the material particles.

I'm not interested in finding answers anymore, not in the slightest. For now the questions are enough, and maybe I don't even need them. The discourse has taken this form today precisely because of the things I lack, because for a few moments I glimpsed those fragments of memory, of the soul's memory, and for a few moments I remembered myself. Meanwhile the rest of my life, outside those moments, grows ever more insubstantial.

January 9

A dream bursts into the empty discourse:

I'm in a bed in a large room, accompanied by two women. One of them is Alicia, who's lying on my left, her feet level with my head. On my right, the same way around as me, is X (whom I met many years ago, and who these days is an old woman, though in the dream she looked young). Fresh, joyous sexual desire flows between the three of us, although Alicia remains slightly apart. She doesn't disapprove; instead she's smiling, hoping her moment will come. The room, however, is very much open to onlookers, with a large window on the right and large glass doors on the left, and at one point Ignacio appears, stops outside the door, and tries to come in. I send him away and shut the door, and I also start closing the blinds and lowering the curtains to protect us from any observers, whether from the left side or the right. I go back to my place in the bed and X uncovers her breasts to be stroked. And now there's a sudden change of scene: we're on a beach and Alicia is shouting the name of a celebrity (someone who was popular some years ago but must be completely forgotten by now, a pop musician or a singer). I look up and see a man in sunglasses coming over to say hello. X and I are rather put out at this interruption, whereas Alicia seems to think it's extremely important to have him there, if only to temporarily halt our games. Eventually X turns around; she has her back to me now and is looking forlorn, so I stop worrying about what's going on around us and focus on fondling her breasts, pressing my body against hers. There the scene fades out, but more as if I'm sinking into a deeper slumber than waking up.

In another of the dream's story lines, my mother may not have been personally present, but it's clear I was trying (literally) to "cut the cord." I don't know when or why, but I'd collected some very long ropes and made them into a single rope that reached across the street and into a building on the other side. This longer rope seemed to have served its purpose and it was time to cut it, so I was looking around for a knife (a serrated one, like a kitchen knife). When tying the ropes together, my sort of structure in the pre-move chaos. But to be genuinely useful as discipline, these exercises need to be about forming the letters first and foremost, without me getting carried away by the contents of the discourse. My handwriting needs to become larger and, of course, perfectly legible. I breathe deeply in an attempt to calm my nerves, not thinking about all the things I have to do, but since really I can't stop thinking about them, it doesn't matter what I write. I need to pack up my books—put them all into neat piles, that is, and tie them with pieces of string. I also need to watch a considerable number of videos, some because they relate to work I'm doing, and some to make sure we get our money's worth after renting the VCR. There are other move-related things I need to sort out as well. I don't know exactly what they are, but I should. I'll need to think about them, then, and make a list. I should also spend a bit of time officially entering 1991, bringing my schedule up to date, and I need to buy a diary for this year. Then I have to, or I ought to, get ready to publish, or to attempt to publish, a few books. But since it's quite clear that I don't have enough time, I choose to wash my hands of everything and play on the computer instead.

January 13

Yesterday's handwriting exercises certainly helped me concentrate on the things I have to do, and I even managed to start organizing and tying up my books without despairing too much. Writing this is rather uncomfortable, though, because when I took the books off the shelves, they brought with them a shower of paint and plaster chippings from the wall, which had been building up on top of them for a considerable time. Many of these tiny specks are now underneath this piece of paper, getting on my nerves and making my work more difficult. I don't know why I didn't think to wipe the table top (I seem to remember it's tabletop rather than table top). I don't know why I don't do it now. But I carry on writing.

G G G G G G G G G G G G Great, I forgot how to do the G again. My problem is that I can never remember where to start, and if it doesn't happen naturally then thinking about it gets me nowhere. There must be some knack to it, but I haven't found it yet.

I know my handwriting's awful today. I'm writing very quickly and anxiously; the buildup of tension and worry about the move is huge. I need to keep tying my books into packages, and there are lots of other things to do as well. I don't feel like doing any of it. I don't want to move. I'm sick of moves and changes. But it has to be done, because the powers that be have decreed it.

January 15

Although these exercises seem like a somewhat inappropriate task under the circumstances, I immerse myself in them, looking for my center—which by the way I'm not going to find, though I can at least try to get close. I notice I've had big handwriting from the get-go today, and although it's not exactly beautiful, it's not ugly either. This could be thanks to the small amount of wine I had at lunchtime. I also notice that I never get the *x* right; I can't seem to master it, perhaps because of the problem of drawing the second line without lifting the pen. Let's see: for e*x*ample, for e*x*ample, for e*x*ample . . . that's how it should be, and I think it's possible only if you draw the second line after you write the whole word, like the dot of an i or the cross of a t, going back and checking the word after you've finished writing it to see what extra bits are missing. It's a serious flaw in the handwritten script of our language that it can't be written without lifting the pen, though maybe in other languages it's even worse. But let's go back to the *x:* if I try to write the word in a single movement of the pen, the next thing I know the whole thing's a mess. I also need to remember to relax and save drawing the second line until the end. And now I'm reaching the end of this sheet of paper without having found my center or anything like it, though at least my writing is large and easy to read.

February 4

I'm trying to get back into a good habit, which is almost as hard as getting out of a bad one. And I'm still paralyzed, in many respects, because of the move and everything that came with it. In the chaos of recent days, in the constant frantic struggle to find and attempt to secure a little order, I've had neither the space, the time, nor the mental capacity for any other kind of work. Things still aren't in their final places, and there's a lot, and I mean a lot, to be done in the new house, but some kind of system has been restored, at least in terms of space. Time is still messy and unstructured, and I suspect this lack of structure in my time is leading to a similar lack of structure in my conscious self. It's hard to feel connected to myself, not just in the profound sense, but in small ways and small everyday actions. You are yourself, but you're also your environment; the self is extended and projected into its surroundings, and any disruption there disrupts the whole psyche.

Part Three: Exercises

February 18, 1991

I'm returning to these exercises today in a vain attempt to gather up the floating pieces of myself. But this isn't the right kind of pen for this paper. The ink's running. I pick up the ballpoint instead, and these departures from my routine are a clear sign of fragmentation. So many—*so* many—things need tidying up (or, more accurately, sorting out) in the new house, and in myself and the people around me, that it's quite overwhelming. And there's the imminent journey to Montevideo, and probably from there to Maldonado, which is making everything feel much more chaotic. My position is that I simply cannot, and should not, make the journey, that the cost (psychologically speaking) would be too great. There's no way out of it, though, and the cost of not going would be even greater. It's the sort of situation that makes you schizophrenic, and which Laing calls a "position of checkmate." (And there's no one like a mother for creating these situations. She says, and believes, that she broke her hip because a gust of wind knocked her over. I, however, am convinced the wind came from her unconscious: a final, desperate effort to bring me to her side.) These days, my misfortunes weigh on me more heavily than ever before. My lack of freedom is total and I can feel time racing by at full tilt, dispiriting and fruitless. The anxiety building inside me is impossible to control. I'm putting on weight; my body's getting more bloated by the day. And I smoke without stopping—and without enjoying it.

I have no idea how to deal with all this, and all the while my desk is spilling over with things to do. There are things, too, that I have to do for myself, for pleasure, or to remind myself who I am, to subsist and exist—and I can't do them. I can't even create the necessary conditions in which to do them.

March 15

Today's exercises are like a branch I'm clinging onto after falling off a cliff. I've never been in such a desperate situation as this, though I've had plenty of difficult times over the years. At least before, there was a deep-down, "magical" confidence that kept me going, a secret, mysterious presence within me like a kind of guardian angel. Beneath everything else, I had a hidden and convoluted confidence in myself, and an even more hidden and convoluted confidence in God. And that confidence always sustained me. Now it's as if I've lost my footing completely; my mind is fragmented and I'm in the grip of a psychological paralysis that, little by little, is becoming physical as well. <u>Nothing</u> about the present looks like happiness, not for a moment; there's no peace or respite, no dreams to remember—my spirit's like an arid pasture, a desert. And there's not the slightest glimmer of a future, of any desirable future whatsoever. The whole thing feels like I'm hurling myself vertiginously downward through days, weeks, months, and years that pass without a trace, completely empty of content, toward death, the only certainty. Every day, for too long now, all I've been able to do is passively observe the progress of my ruin.

This is all very abstract, I know. It's not that I can't be more specific, but I'm tired of being more specific, and I don't want to repeat myself. After all, this is just a handwriting exercise. There's no point worrying about making its contents more concrete. It's just filling a sheet of paper with my writing.

March 17

I need to establish some form of discipline, however hard that may be. These exercises are always the first step in my attempts to do that—attempts that normally never get anywhere. And yet I keep on beginning with these exercises, partly because they're the simplest way to begin. All you need is a ballpoint and a sheet of paper, whereas everything else—everything else I might want to do—means first carrying out a search for the necessary equipment, which puts me off before I've even started. Calligraphical exercises can also be done anywhere, though it's still not easy to find an appropriate place for them in the new house, since all the possibilities have very serious potential drawbacks. For example, I'm now sitting at my desk in the room next to the first-floor bedroom; this spot can only be used on a day like today, when there's a cool breeze. Otherwise, the temperature in here is unbearable at almost all hours of the day or night because of a zinc roof that's lacking the proper insulation. It's also very small, and there's no space for my stuff; even as I write, papers and other bits and pieces on the desk are getting in my way, and I can't put them anywhere else because there's nowhere else for them and no suitable furniture. I can think of lots of reasons why my handwriting's so bad today, among them the fact that I haven't practiced much lately, but I'm also feeling unsettled and obstructed by the untidiness of the desk. Other simple tasks have become nightmarish, because to do them I have to go and get things from the back bedroom, where all the stuff is in precarious piles and the unpleasant climate is very off-putting.

March 18

At last, two days of exercises in a row. I've even managed to do a few odd jobs inside and outside the house. The major problem of having nowhere to work hasn't gone away, though, and this morning the buzzing from the electricity substation next door reached extraordinary volumes. It woke me up and tortured me at great length, until finally I dragged myself out of bed; downstairs, the noise filled the whole house, with the exception of Ignacio's room. There are no two ways about it: my only option is to move in there until somewhere else has been set up for me. Ignacio doesn't like the idea, but he'll have to accept it.

Ignacio is getting more difficult by the day. I think there are a few reasons for this, among them his mother's almost constant absence, the maid's lack of authority over him, and the fact that he has a house key and a room that looks onto the street, meaning his friends are forever tempting him out. Today I threatened to make him move into the little room at the back of the house, which would keep him away from the lure of the street and allow us (or rather, me) to control him better. It would be a cruel step to take, since it's extremely uncomfortable in there. But it's something to bear in mind, in case things don't improve and Ignacio turns out to be incapable of even a modicum of self-control. He's still like a small animal with no moral code, always doing whatever he feels like doing and whatever he thinks is best for him. For a while his behavior was getting better, but since the move and the arrival of the new maid it's gone downhill, and fast. I hope I can find a way to get him back on track, but I'm very tired.

March 19

Third consecutive day of calligraphical exercises. This is like a small light shining in the darkness (of my mind). I'm also pleased to see my handwriting looking more even. It's still a bit small; I'll try to make it bigger, but I don't want to force things too much. It's better to let my being express itself in whatever way it can, even if the actual handwriting and the desired therapeutic effects suffer as a result. The important thing for now is getting out of my catatonic state; it doesn't matter whether I make an elegant exit. All I'm asking of myself, all I've begun asking, and even demanding, of myself, is action. It might be action like this—writing a modest couple of pages—or it might be venturing into the outside world, if only to walk a couple of blocks to buy cigarettes. I need to fight against my phobias, and against stasis and passivity, especially because this passivity is harboring a potent destructive force. It would be better to smash things up—to do anything else whatsoever—than to carry on in this senseless limbo in which *nothing* will ever be fixed and I'll just get angrier and more frustrated. My anger isn't directed at anyone in particular by now, except, I think, myself. It's true that my circumstances are a pileup of disasters and difficult situations, but it's my own inadequate response to them—slow, clumsy, and uncertain—that makes them worse, and makes the possibility of solutions seem further and further away.

March 20

Fourth consecutive day of exercises. Although I'm sitting in the midst of the maddening buzz from the machines next door, I'm trying to follow the guidance Alicia gave me when I woke up. Strangely enough, this guidance is based on my own words, written as part of yesterday's exercises, which she read before going to sleep, or maybe once she was already dozing off. I'd said I wasn't responding to problems in the right way and that I needed to change that. Alicia said the same thing to me this morning, and added a few practical suggestions of her own. She must not have remembered what she read of my exercises last night.

I have good intentions, but the problem of the buzzing, which aggravates or multiplies the suffering already caused by all the other post-move problems, such as the heat, the lack of defense against the heat, and the lack of space, gets more intolerable by the day. At this moment, the buzzing has reached an astounding intensity; it's even competing with the noise from the street. And it's right in the middle of where I'm sitting to work. It's filling the space, getting louder and louder, and there's no point closing the doors and windows: now I can feel it in the form of vibrations in the soles of my feet, which are resting—encased in their slippers—on the wooden floor. It's like an infuriating vibromassage. My good intentions aren't going to be enough. I'm desperate to get out of here; I'm writing as fast as I can in order to finish the page at once and make a run for it. HELP.

March 21

Fifth consecutive day of exercises. The good news is, they seem to have become a habit by now. Of course, they're still a long way from calligraphical exercises carried out with concentration and diligence, but we mustn't expect too much. (Today I read a tremendous bit of Rilke, along the lines of: "Reality is something distant, coming infinitely slowly to those who are patient.") (Let us be patient, then, and wait for that distant thing to come.)

(But few things conspire more against patience, and therefore against reality, than this constant buzzing that won't let me sleep, think, or pay attention to anything else. And then there's the interminably unsettled weather, heavy, humid, and with low air pressure. A storm's been brewing for days now, but it won't make up its mind to start, which sets the nerves on edge and makes it hard to get anything done. We've had the occasional patch of begrudging, monotonous drizzle over the past few days, but what we really need is a violent explosion of lightning, thunder, and wind, an elemental fury to release all the static electricity building up in the earth, people, and things.)

But I'm getting increasingly carried away by my narrative urges and forgetting about my handwriting. Now I'm paying more attention to the writing, but my hand's rushing nervously to form the letters without leaving my thoughts any time for reflection. The buzzing has gone, and the room where I'm working is reasonably cool. But Alicia is calling me.

March 23

Yesterday I skipped these exercises. Today I've decided to come back to them, in spite of the weather conditions, which are even worse than they were yesterday. At least right now there's no noticeable buzzing—except in my own ears, where there's a high-pitched humming sound I often hear inside my head when I'm not sleeping enough. Speaking of which, ever since the buzzing from the substation next door began, my sleep's been terrible: I have trouble nodding off and wake up constantly throughout the night. This puts me in a bad mood and makes me irritable, demotivated, and unable to do even the simplest things. I've also had to make do with sleeping on the fly, as it were, seizing my chance whenever somewhere free of buzzing also happens to be free of people. This is all very bad for my health. My main comfort is reading, for the most part books I've already read more than once. Reading is a way of distancing myself a little from the buzzing and from my awareness of my own discomfort. I also need to distance myself from the bustle and mess of this house, which, in part because of my low morale, is no closer to being sorted out. The other people who live or work here haven't done anything either. Yesterday I dreamed I lived day and night on a long-distance bus, which isn't a bad image to describe my instability and the feelings of insecurity this situation is causing me. And now it's almost Holy Week, or Tourism Week, and of course all the activity in the country has come to a halt. So the search for solutions to my problems has also been called off for the time being.

March 25

Today is a strange day in many ways. For example, the weather conditions are very mixed-up and volatile, as if summer were happening at the same time as autumn; it's cold and hot, with changeable air pressure, all of which disturbs the body and leads to a vague feeling of unease. What's more, today I woke up to the news that there's been a murder in Colonia, in one of the pleasant spots we often visit. A murder in a detective novel is one thing, but it's something else entirely in so-called real life. It's not nice to think of living in a small, trusting, and very unprotected town with a murderer on the loose. Or more than one by now, since the victim was a woman and there are also suspicions of rape. Today is also strange because of the news that one of my books is probably going to be published in Belgium, and the even stranger news that they might pay a considerable advance for the rights.

As for the weather, if it really has settled down into a fairly normal autumn at last, perhaps I'll be able to get back to work, even before I make the changes I've planned around the house so I can keep all my things together in one place. Once the stifling heat goes away, I'll feel physically and mentally stronger, able to overcome the problems and irritations of not having a space of my own.

March 26

The atmosphere today (meteorologically speaking) is very conducive to work. There's a cool breeze—too cool at times—and yesterday's mixture of seasons and temperatures has gone. The electricity board also seems to have solved (though not completely definitively) the problem of the buzzing, which has gotten rid of another paralyzing factor. The problem of finding a space of my own remains, but steps are being taken to create one for me. As for the buzzing, I must have been sensitized to it by now, because every so often I feel like I can hear it as loudly as before. All it takes is any other sound—the engine of a car, a motorcycle, or even the fridge—making a similar impression on my ear for that impression to become prolonged and amplified and then frighten me by turning into that same permanent buzzing. It's clear the buzzing hasn't completely disappeared and that the walls of the house are transmitting it continuously. I don't know if this level of sound has been here all along and I'm only noticing it now, when I listen closely in certain strategic locations, because I've been sensitized to it, or if the real problem hasn't fully been solved. Time will tell, I suppose, since when a stimulus goes away the sensitivity to that stimulus gradually decreases until it reaches the normal threshold of perception.

In today's exercises, I've taken care to make my handwriting legible, but I'm still a long way from the patience and concentration necessary to achieve the results I'm aiming for.

March 27

The buzzing is back, at full blast. I find the whole thing very strange. It's the second time this has happened: the workmen come and do some repairs, and the repairs last for a total of precisely twenty-four hours. The only thing I can think of to compare it with is the problem of the noise from the fridge. Sometimes a loose panel starts vibrating with the movement of the motor, and the sound builds until what's usually a soft purring becomes quite intolerable. Then I go and slide some cardboard into a suitable position between the loose panel and the body of the fridge to stop the rattling. But after a few days, or a few hours, the vibrations dislodge the cardboard and it ends up in a place where it has absolutely no impact on the noise, and the whole thing starts again. I think something similar must happen with the machines in the substation; the workmen come along with some quick fix, not so different from mine with the fridge, then the vibrations themselves render it null and void. We need a permanent solution. With the fridge, putting a few screws in would probably do it. As for those machines, I don't know what the solution would be, but we need to keep demanding one. No one can live under these conditions.

April 1

Juan Ignacio is now at soccer practice, Alicia is at work, and the maid is at home (or wherever she is—she's not here, anyway); the Holy Week guests have now left; it's now 7:30 p.m., the walls are exuding no buzzing noise whatsoever, and I even managed to doze off for a few minutes; I've now been for a walk on the beach with Alicia and felt how my body is deteriorating; I've had breakfast and lunch and a snack and cleaned my teeth three times; it's now no longer too hot, in fact it's pleasantly cool; the dog isn't barking and there's nobody at the door; the working day is now over, or almost over, for many people. And so I can now sit at my desk and, after so many days of total inertia, begin these exercises again.

I'll start paying attention to my handwriting now; I knew it was bad from the outset, but I was in a hurry to get down what I was feeling. From here on in I can start to expect a bit more of myself and begin thinking about the shapes of the letters. I don't think I'll ever manage to write legibly and quickly at the same time; // I've just been interrupted, first by the doorbell and then by the phone//. Not too long from now, I hope to have sorted out a place to work. Then I'll be able to get down to these exercises, and everything else, in earnest.

April 3

I'm searching for and discovering strategies that might help me survive this strange state of marginalization within my own home. Yesterday I managed a good siesta, making the most of a pause in the buzzing, and at night I found a mysterious spot in the bedroom where the vibratory waves canceled each other out, creating a hollow of silence, or relative silence, where I could sleep. I suspect the battle against the noise won't be over as quickly as it seemed, though; the electricity board claims they're going to solve the problem once and for all "today or tomorrow" by removing the faulty machine, but they've said that before without anything changing. Maybe we'll end up in court. We'll see. Another factor contributing to my marginalization, the maid, is less of a problem now that she's been replaced by a new maid whose presence doesn't radiate aggression and who, conversely, seems interested in cooperation. Still, a house with servants is a "house taken over," or at least a house with ever-changing occupied zones. If in the unaggressive presence of the current maid we could do a few basic things (more water in the tank, doors that close properly, etc.), my marginalization would be easier to bear. There would still be the presence of Ignacio, with his intrusive curiosity about everything I do. In his case, the educative efforts will need to be intensive and immediate. There's also the problem of Alicia and her unpredictable hours, but I don't think that problem has a solution. My marginalization will always ultimately be sustained by her, even if everything else can be happily resolved. Nevertheless, there's hope that I might be able to start work again, in a future that doesn't seem too distant or impossible to reach.

April 7

WARNING: This handwriting exercise contains scenes the reader may find distressing.

It's about Pongo the dog, whom I've said on several occasions we need to get rid of. My reasons for this aren't emotional; they're based entirely on logic and reason, and today something happened to add fuel to my arguments. I'd been out in the back garden with Pongo for a while, playing with the ping-pong ball (which he completely destroyed), and we'd even had one of our usual sessions of cuddles and affectionate words. Then Pongo the dog went over to a spot very close to his lair among the hortensias, and when I followed him I saw to my horror that he'd gotten ahold of a small piece of rotten meat. He'd probably buried it a few days before. Some time ago, I'd found a big piece of meat in the garden covered in soil, but it wasn't rotten, perhaps because it was almost entirely coated in a layer of fat, and after I'd dug it up Pongo hadn't shown the slightest interest in it. But standing over him now, I saw he'd put this new piece of meat down in a clear patch of ground and was pretending to be lying casually on his back, the way he often does, only this time aiming to have the piece of meat more or less underneath his neck. I made a sound he recognizes as disapproving and he stopped what he was doing; when I looked more closely, I spotted two or three little white conical maggots on the ground (shaped like truncated cones, and similar to the ones I once found in the cap of an empty bottle of floor wax, though much bigger and fatter). Then I saw, disgusted, that the piece of meat Pongo had dug up was covered in the very same maggots.

(second sheet)

Pongo the dog was on the alert, guarding the piece of meat. He growled when I tried to pick it up with the shovel and poker from the outdoor stove and even grabbed it in his teeth to take it away somewhere safe. I gave him a severe telling-off, at which point he let go and stood a few feet away, letting me do what I wanted but not taking his eyes off me. I carried the hunk of meat to the stove along with the fat-covered piece I'd found before, doused them both with methylated spirits, and set them alight, feeding the flames with some newspaper and twigs, and later with a couple of logs. Flies of all sizes were soon lured over by the smell of the roasting meat, fat, and maggots, and they even flew inside the stove and darted around looking for the source (though without getting as close to the flames as I would have liked).

It wasn't easy to keep the fire hot enough for the meat to carbonize. I had to add more methylated spirits a couple of times, but eventually the process seemed complete. The flies disappeared, though the sickening stench—which is also the sickening stench of Pongo himself when he smells bad—clung to my nostrils for a long time afterwards, even during a foray into the outside world in search of some coffee.

All the while, I kept asking myself what could have possessed Pongo to do something so disgusting; whether its purpose was medicinal (to make his fur healthier, kill parasites, etc.) or merely cosmetic, that is, as a kind of perfume to attract members of the opposite sex with dubious olfactory preferences. I've also noticed there's a similar smell in the vicinity of the hortensias permanently now. I think Pongo is creating a kind of private graveyard in the back garden, burying pieces of meat all over the place. WE NEED TO GET RID OF HIM IMMEDIATELY.

April 9

It looks like we're reaching the final stages of this nightmare, and within a few days I'll be able to begin going back, little by little, to my "normal" life (I use quotation marks because I know full well that my life has never been normal, thank God). I don't want to be too optimistic, but the latest news about the buzzing seems promising. The problem could be completely gone by tomorrow. (And at this very moment, as if someone's watching what I'm writing so they can make fun of me—so they can hit me where it really hurts—the buzzing has started up at full volume.) (I'm trying to keep calm, but my left ear's still aching from the awful vibrations yesterday and this morning.) I'd be better off finishing these exercises with no further pretensions of neatness and swiftly escaping into a less affected part of the house.

All the work (or the most important parts of it, at least) that needs doing to turn the garage into a space I can use is either arranged or in progress, and dates have been agreed upon for the completion of each stage. Allowing for any potential setbacks or delays in the workmen's activities, I should—I hope—be installed in there no later than the middle of next week. Meanwhile, I have some pressing work to do (going through the edits of *Fauna* for the Belgian publisher) which can't be delayed, so I'll attempt to make a start right now——in spite of everything.

. . . .

. . . .

. . . .

. . . .

. . . .

. . . .

August 24

Another attempt—this is like the myth of Sisyphus—to get back into habits that are good for my health, such as doing my handwriting exercises. Today I also went for a walk around the port. It used to be my usual route, but recently I gave up going for regular walks, along with everything else. The main idea at the moment, generally speaking, is to force myself a little (as much as I can) to keep doing good things, so they turn into habits and replace my other habits. Here's a brief list of the habits I'm trying to replace: (1) excessive smoking, (2) valium, (3) watching too many films on video, (4) playing with electronic machines, (5) excessive reading, especially at strange hours of the day or night.

To mask, moderate, or banish these habits, I propose: (1) returning to these exercises, (2) going for walks again, (3) persevering with the challenge of making myself relax or meditate for a few minutes each day, (4) going to the gym on a daily basis again, (5) spending more time in my garage-office, with or without music, working or not, (6) returning to my games of ping-pong with Juan Ignacio.

My handwriting's looking pretty awful. I should probably add to my resolutions: (7) trying to do these exercises calmly and with full dedication (even though I notice that at this moment my hand is completely out of control).

As expected, Alicia has come to interrupt me before the agreed-upon time, which means I can't finish this page in peace. I'll need to make a particular effort to eliminate unnecessary interruptions from now on. I've had some success so far, by turning off the telephone ringer in the bedroom and the garage. But I have to instill a sense of respect for my privacy, personal space, and need for concentration in the other members of this household.

August 27

The aim today is to manage my anxiety and make my handwriting large and clear. So I'm going slowly, trying not to give in to the current of thoughts I can feel bursting to express something, not because I don't think I should be expressing anything, but because I don't want the current to carry me away (for example, when I wrote the word "current" just then, my writing sped up anxiously, and as a result the r's didn't come out right. Current. Current). (The thing is, when you write one r, you think that ought to be enough, and then you rush the next one because a second r seems like a luxury with no purpose other than slowing you down and interrupting the rhythm of the writing.) But in general I'm quite pleased with how today's exercises are going. My handwriting had become so scrambled and microscopic that deep down I was beginning to despair of ever turning it back into a legible script; specifically, the legible script I'd managed after weeks and months of more or less daily exercises. But I'm delighted to see that the exercises I did the day before yesterday were enough to help me identify the bad habits in my writing, allowing today's progress to take shape within me unconsciously in the time that's passed since then. I dare anyone to tell me that what I'm writing now isn't perfectly legible, even if it's a long way from anything that might be called "calligraphy." I'm not aiming for calligraphy, though; I'd be content with handwriting that I, and other people, could easily read, without it needing to reach any level of beauty or perfection. The French refrain puts it well: "Le meilleur c'est l'ennemi du bon," as M. V. instilled in me. But there are plenty of strokes I still need to improve, and I should also work on writing more quickly without sacrificing quality.

August 28

I'm determined to keep these exercises as exercises and nothing more, rather than seeing them as a useful way of expressing things I'm feeling, thinking, or experiencing. The priority is the handwriting, I know; I need to learn to form the letters before moving on to any other stages. Because the hand forming the letters needs to become confident first and foremost, and then loose and fast-moving, and this confidence comes from a feeling of certainty; that is, you can't start hesitating because you're worried about what the handwriting looks like. It, the handwriting, like the way of joining one letter to the next, should follow a single, preestablished pattern and not be made up as you go along. For example, I know I have trouble with the r because of habits I've developed over years of writing it the wrong way, without all the features that make it easy to identify immediately. My r's are identified more by their position in the word (and look at that badly written r in the word "word").

A particularly appropriate activity at this stage, then, would be to deliberately write words with r's in them. Round and round the rugged rock the ragged rascal ran (was there a second line? I don't remember). Round and round the rugged rock the ragged rascal ran. But I'll get bored if I keep repeating the same thing, so I need to think of other words with r's in them beyond that silly tongue twister. For example, rhododendron, rower, sombrero, bra-strap, parricide, reverberate, procrastinate, corduroys (I repeat: corduroys). (I don't know why this word comes out so badly: corduroys, ~~cor~~ corduroys, that's better, corduroys, corduroys.) Raspberry, crosscurrents, crosscurrents, extracurricular, extracurricular, extracurricular, extracurricular. Transferrable. Transferrable, transferrable, transfer, transfer, transfer, transfer, transfer. It's still not right.

August 29

Relaxing the hand and ~~forming fo~~ forming each letter with love; that's today's motto. I've noticed that my hand and arm are often tense when I write. If I did any more than the page I currently fill with these exercises, I could easily end up with so-called writer's cramp. Trying to relax the muscles might lead to a decline in the quality of the output, but I think it's a stage I have to go through, because my previous achievements, though considerable, came from focusing on the wrong part of the problem. So my writing might look careless and untidy at the moment, but this is actually due to a deliberate attempt on my part to change the way I work, which is no easy task because it involves keeping my attention strictly divided between the tension in my muscles (now they relax, now I get distracted and they tense up, and so on) and the act in itself of ~~forming formi~~ forming the letters. It's difficult, very difficult indeed, but I think it's the right approach. Keeping an eye on the tension in my muscles is also useful training for my plan to make relaxation a daily habit, which is something I'm always putting off but can put off no longer because it's a crucial part of good health—or of my good health, at least. According to my theory, ~~rel~~ relaxation leads to the production of endorphins, which will allow me to smoke less, for one thing, and might eventually help me stop smoking altogether (something else I've been putting off for too long).

August 30

And so I continue with my new approach, keeping the muscles in my arm and hand relaxed. Let's see if I can manage some passable handwriting under these conditions. It looks like I can. The secret is relaxing the muscles selectively, so only the ones that are absolutely essential to holding the ballpoint are active, while all the others (in my hand and arm but also in the rest of my body) remain as loose as possible. It's difficult, I know. But it can be done. I need to stop for a second, though, because Pongo the dog is barking outside and waiting for me to open the door (another new development since the move is my role as doorman, since there's no gap in the wire fence here to let him in and out as he pleases).

*

I'm back. Relaxing isn't easy at the best of times, and it's even harder when you've just kicked the dog. These days he likes to wait until you open the door for him, and then, instead of coming in, run off and bark furiously at the passersby, as if he needed your protective presence to do so. You end up standing by the open door like a fool, waiting until His Lordship decides he's barked enough and deigns to come back. He knows this behavior gets him a kicking, so he scurries inside very quickly and nervously, trying to move faster than the oncoming foot. Sometimes he manages it, but not today.

Recounting this distracted me from my muscles and careful *~~forming for~~* forming of the letters. I can't let myself get overexcited by telling stories; I need to focus on the real reason for doing these exercises. At least today I managed to relax enough to begin distinguishing between the muscles I should be relaxing and those I shouldn't.

September 5

I have a good excuse for neglecting these exercises (in their appealing, encouraging, relaxing new incarnation) over the past several days, since I urgently needed to put together a collection of short stories—but now I'm getting distracted from forming the letters properly.

Preparing this collection of stories, I was going to say, was a demanding and even rather torturous process involving selecting the texts, some of which had been lost years ago in envelopes containing other things; making decisions (this one yes, this one no; I prefer this version to that, and so on); tracking down the details of previous publications (if there were any); and photocopying the final version of some texts, etc.; and all within a very tight time frame, something like three days. But now I'm getting distracted from forming the letters again.

I need to pay close attention to my handwriting—and indeed to my hand, bearing in mind which muscles I have to keep tense and which I have to relax. Since it's impossible to concentrate on everything at once, I need to achieve a kind of oscillating attention, which ~~swi~~ swings between one thing and the other, until one day, I imagine, my movements (i.e., the regular handwriting and the selective ~~relaxation~~ relaxation) will become automatic. In the meantime, I need to practice and practice, and even if I don't think I'll ~~manage~~ manage more than my usual daily page, it at least needs to be every day, without missing any the way I ~~normally~~ normally do when faced with external obligations that often seem urgent and essential, though of course they hardly ever are. That's enough for today, but I'll be back.

September 6

I should be having lunch right now, but I think practicing my relaxation and meticulous handwriting is more important for my psychosomatic health. So, since later on I'll get caught up, as always, in a chain of events that have nothing to do with me, and I won't find the moments of calm that are indispensable/indispensable (I repeat the word because I've noticed I tend to rush long words and don't pay attention to forming each letter); indispensable, I was saying (and I'll say it again: indispensable), for the intense mental concentration that ~~exerc~~ exercises like these require, I decided to prioritize this activity and put off—at no small personal sacrifice—my lunch. T T That was a very long and complicated sentence. It's nice to see that today I'm keeping the muscles in my hand and arm that aren't used for writing relatively relaxed, and that, at the same time, my handwriting's quite even (~~compared~~ compared with previous days, when I'd only just adopted this approach). Now I have to extend the relaxation, little by little, to the rest of my ~~body~~ ~~body~~ body, which will be no small feat.

September 7

Concentration. Relaxation. Focus on forming the letters and focus on your muscles. The only ones you should be using are the ones involved in holding the ballpoint and ~~moving~~ moving it as you write; that is, the muscles in the thumb, index finger, and middle finger of the right hand, and the muscles in the wrist (which seem to affect the little finger) and the forearm, which needs to glide slowly over the surface of the desk. The biceps also do ~~so~~ some work (I can feel it), but I don't know if they're supposed to or if it's just a needless contraction. The rest of the muscles in my body should be relaxed, but they're not. This is called tension, and it's what I have to work on correcting, while my ~~ha~~ hand's unhurried activity becomes automatic. For too long now I've been unable to loosen up, at least as completely as I used to be able to.

I'm carrying on after an interruption (an in no way uncommon occurrence in this house) (and one of the reasons why I can't loosen up properly). Now another interruption. This house is hardly a monastery of monks bound by a vow of silence.

The situation, however, is less serious than at other points in my life, for example the period I went through about ten years ago, even if it's more serious in terms of the internal factors that keep me from relaxing. And I'm putting my faith in these exercises, at least as a starting point. Today I managed to pay attention to both arms as I was writing, though I didn't form the letters so well as a result.

September 8

And even though it's Sunday, here I am, present and ready to maintain the continuity of these relaxed (in the good sense of the word) exercises. I'm monitoring the muscular tension in my fingers; I want to feel that only the muscles which should be working are doing so. When it comes to my writing arm, I still have problems with the unintentional contraction of the bicep (or biceps?), which for some reason seems to be linked to the middle finger (maybe it is; I should ask Alicia if she remembers the relevant insertions).

But now look: because I've been paying attention to my ~~muscles~~ muscles, I've neglected my handwriting. I was also distracted by the memory of a surprising discovery I made yesterday afternoon during my siesta: namely, that I find the sensation of being relaxed, especially when accompanied by a marked tranquility of mind, profoundly unpleasant.

This discovery left me concerned and bewildered, since I'm deliberately pursuing ~~rela~~ relaxation and peace of mind and wondering why I can't achieve them. The obvious, practical answer that ~~stru~~ struck me yesterday is this: I'm not achieving them because I don't want to achieve them.

Then I reached the conclusion that my experiences over the past few years (Buenos Aires, family life) have changed the addiction I used to have to endorphins (which I'd developed with hard work and support) into an addiction to adrenaline, and my inclination toward alpha waves has shifted toward beta waves. This is all very worrying, but I shouldn't lose hope, and, as Alicia always says, I need to find the halfway point, the balance. I must try to create a space for—a shift, however slight, toward—endorphins (especially since with time they can replace the need for nicotine). To be continued.

September 19

I know it's been days and days since I last did these ~~exercises~~ exercises—I abandoned them when I was feeling particularly crazy and anxious. Today I'm still feeling crazy and anxious, but I'm also determined to start sorting things out. Going back to these exercises is always the first step toward psychophysical health, I think, though obviously they're not enough by themselves, and there are plenty of other areas of my life that need addressing as well. And that's what I'm going to try to do, plugging my ears with wax so I don't hear the song of the sirens who want to lure me from the true path (in ~~fact~~ fact, my ears are plugged with wax anyway at the moment, as usually happens to me every other winter).

I should add that I'm amazed at the quality of the handwriting on this page—I would have expected it to be much smaller and more uneven. It's actually fairly easy to read, which I find astonishing. I should also say that I'm not bothering to relax the muscles that don't need to be tense while I'm writing, though I haven't forgotten about that. Every day ~~I pray~~ I pray to God for the strength and reason I'll need in my determined pursuit of discipline in all these areas of my life. Ciao.

September 20

I hope I'm not interrupted during these exercises, though I can't say I feel very optimistic. All right, I'll begin by getting more settled in my chair, resting my feet comfortably on the floor and my left ~~arm~~ ~~arm~~ arm on the desk, trying to relax from the shoulder down. Next I focus my attention on my right hand, trying to sense the muscles that need to be active and relax the others, in the wrist, and now in the rest of the arm, and also from the ~~shoulder~~ shoulder. Now let's think about the handwriting: I need to slow down the rhythm, which is currently too fast, and find the patience to form each ~~letter~~ letter as correctly as possible. I have trouble writing any more slowly than this, but

*

The asterisk indicates that I was indeed interrupted (a few hours ~~ago~~ ago), and now (~~very late at n~~ at almost one in the morning) I doubt I'll be able to continue these exercises as determinedly as I began them. I'll try to go on with the calligraphical part, at least, without worrying about relaxing my muscles; now I'm slowing down————trying to slow down——the rhythm of my writing and concentrating on each of the letters. I'm also trying to forget, as much as I can, about the coherence of what I'm saying. I'm thinking about each letter in turn—but everything I just wrote is in fact completely untrue; I'm still going too fast, far too fast, maybe because I can see I'm coming to the end of the page, which normally makes people hurry, as if hurrying could somehow increase the number of words that fit on a piece of paper. But tomorrow is another day.

September 22

When I wrote the date at the top of today's exercises (it's 3:08 p.m. and fewer than twelve hours have passed since yesterday's)—when I wrote the date, as I was saying, I realized a lot of things about my behavior last night and my current uneasy state. Today is my mother's birthday. She passed away ~~five~~ five weeks ago. It's Sunday now, and last Saturday I was with Alicia at the cemetery, marking the first month since her death. I don't normally go in for these things, but this is an exceptional case, firstly because one's mother is always someone particularly important, but also because this ~~death~~ death brings with it real reasons—not just unconscious, fantastical ones—for me to feel guilty, and this guilt is very difficult to overcome. I even resorted to confessing to a ~~priest~~ priest, which was highly uncharacteristic of me. It's certainly true, as the priest helped me see, that my feelings of guilt are exaggerated and based on unverifiable hypotheses about how different things might have been if I'd done x, y, or z. It's also true that I was "made" to be very susceptible to guilt and that the person who made me this way was none other than my mother. But be that as it may, I'm still feeling uneasy, though I've tried to escape that feeling by watching an excessive number of films and to escape myself using other techniques, evasion tactics I adopted during my mother's months of intense suffering and continued to make use of after her death. Now I think it's time to turn back toward myself, to walk the other way down the path of ~~avoidance~~ avoidance, and to trust in the fact that even if I am at fault, I've been forgiven by my mother and by God. As everyone knows, guilt gets you nowhere and ~~repentance~~ repentance really consists of "not sinning again"—of not returning over and over to a previous action you can't undo, and instead returning to normal life and generating good things for yourself and everyone around you, which is better than greeting the world with the ghastly countenance of an invalid. And so, on the seventy-eighth anniversary of her birth, the tribute I owe to my mother is this: my health.

Epilogue: The Empty Discourse

September 22, 1991

When you reach a certain age, you're no longer the protagonist of your own actions: all you have left are the consequences of things you've already done. The seeds you've sown have been growing away, out of sight, and now suddenly they burst up in a kind of jungle that surrounds you on all sides, and you spend your days trying to hack out a path with a machete just so you can breathe. It soon becomes clear that any hope of getting out is completely false, because the jungle's spreading faster than we can cut it back and, more importantly, because the very idea of "getting out" makes no sense: we can't get out because at the same time we don't want to get out, and we don't want to get out because there's nowhere else to go, because the jungle is us and getting out would mean a kind of death, or even death itself. And maybe once we were able to die a certain sort of seemingly harmless death, but now we know such deaths were the seeds we sowed of the jungle we've become.

But today, around sunset, I saw a few reddish rays of sun reflected in some glazed ceramic bricks and realized I'm still alive, in the true sense of the word, and even able to place myself within myself: it's all a question of finding the right balance, by means of a kind of spiritual acrobatics. I can't get free of the tangle of consequences, and there's no point trying to be the protagonist of my own actions again, but what I can do is find my lost self among these new patterns and learn to live again, only differently. There's a way of going with the flow that means you end up in the right place at the right time, and this "going with the flow" is what allows you to be the protagonist of your own actions——when you've reached a certain age.

*

A few days ago, I dreamed about a group of priests in different-colored robes. I remember one of them in particular, whose robes were a very bright purple. They adopted various positions, which in turn combined to form further positions, and I realized they were expressing the secret of Alchemy.

COLONIA, NOVEMBER 1991

COLONIA, MAY 1993

LITERATURE
is not the same thing as
PUBLISHING

Coffee House Press began as a small letterpress operation in 1972 and has grown into an internationally renowned non-profit publisher of literary fiction, essay, poetry, and other work that doesn't fit neatly into genre categories.

Coffee House is both a publisher and an arts organization. Through our *Books in Action* program and publications, we've become interdisciplinary collaborators and incubators for new work and audience experiences. Our vision for the future is one where a publisher is a catalyst and connector.

Funder Acknowledgments

Coffee House Press is an internationally renowned independent book publisher and arts nonprofit based in Minneapolis, MN; through its literary publications and *Books in Action* program, Coffee House acts as a catalyst and connector—between authors and readers, ideas and resources, creativity and community, inspiration and action.

Coffee House Press books are made possible through the generous support of grants and donations from corporations, state and federal grant programs, family foundations, and the many individuals who believe in the transformational power of literature. This activity is made possible by the voters of Minnesota through a Minnesota State Arts Board Operating Support grant, thanks to the legislative appropriation from the Arts and Cultural Heritage Fund. Coffee House also receives major operating support from the Amazon Literary Partnership, the Jerome Foundation, McKnight Foundation, Target Foundation, and the National Endowment for the Arts (NEA). To find out more about how NEA grants impact individuals and communities, visit www.arts.gov.

Coffee House Press receives additional support from the Elmer L. & Eleanor J. Andersen Foundation; the David & Mary Anderson Family Foundation; Bookmobile; Fredrikson & Byron, P.A.; Dorsey & Whitney LLP; the Fringe Foundation; Kenneth Koch Literary Estate; the Knight Foundation; the Matching Grant Program Fund of the Minneapolis Foundation; Mr. Pancks' Fund in memory of Graham Kimpton; the Schwab Charitable Fund; Schwegman, Lundberg & Woessner, P.A.; the Silicon Valley Community Foundation, and the U.S. Bank Foundation.

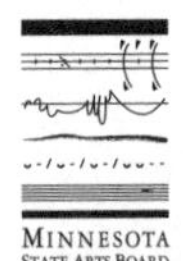

The Publisher's Circle of Coffee House Press

Publisher's Circle members make significant contributions to Coffee House Press's annual giving campaign. Understanding that a strong financial base is necessary for the press to meet the challenges and opportunities that arise each year, this group plays a crucial part in the success of Coffee House's mission.

Recent Publisher's Circle members include many anonymous donors, Suzanne Allen, Patricia A. Beithon, the E. Thomas Binger & Rebecca Rand Fund of the Minneapolis Foundation, Andrew Brantingham, Robert & Gail Buuck, Dave & Kelli Cloutier, Louise Copeland, Jane Dalrymple-Hollo, Mary Ebert & Paul Stembler, Kaywin Feldman & Jim Lutz, Chris Fischbach & Katie Dublinski, Sally French, Jocelyn Hale & Glenn Miller, the Rehael Fund-Roger Hale/Nor Hall of the Minneapolis Foundation, Randy Hartten & Ron Lotz, Dylan Hicks & Nina Hale, William Hardacker, Randall Heath, Jeffrey Hom, Carl & Heidi Horsch, the Amy L. Hubbard & Geoffrey J. Kehoe Fund, Kenneth & Susan Kahn, Stephen & Isabel Keating, Julia Klein, the Kenneth Koch Literary Estate, Cinda Kornblum, Jennifer Kwon Dobbs & Stefan Liess, the Lambert Family Foundation, the Lenfestey Family Foundation, Joy Linsday Crow, Sarah Lutman & Rob Rudolph, the Carol & Aaron Mack Charitable Fund of the Minneapolis Foundation, George & Olga Mack, Joshua Mack & Ron Warren, Gillian McCain, Malcolm S. McDermid & Katie Windle, Mary & Malcolm McDermid, Sjur Midness & Briar Andresen, Maureen Millea Smith & Daniel Smith, Peter Nelson & Jennifer Swenson, Enrique & Jennifer Olivarez, Alan Polsky, Marc Porter & James Hennessy, Robin Preble, Alexis Scott, Ruth Stricker Dayton, Jeffrey Sugerman & Sarah Schultz, Nan G. & Stephen C. Swid, Kenneth Thorp in memory of Allan Kornblum & Rochelle Ratner, Patricia Tilton, Joanne Von Blon, Stu Wilson & Melissa Barker, Warren D. Woessner & Iris C. Freeman, and Margaret Wurtele.

For more information about the Publisher's Circle and other ways to support Coffee House Press books, authors, and activities, please visit www.coffeehousepress.org/pages/support or contact us at info@coffeehousepress.org.

Latin American Translations from Coffee House Press

After the Winter
Guadalupe Nettel
Translated by Rosalind Harvey

Among Strange Victims
Daniel Saldaña París
Translated by Christina MacSweeney

Camanchaca
Diego Zúñiga
Translated by Megan McDowell

Comemadre
Roque Larraquy
Translated by Heather Cleary

Empty Set
Verónica Gerber Bicecci
Translated by Christina MacSweeney

Faces in the Crowd
Valeria Luiselli
Translated by Christina MacSweeney

The Remainder
Alia Trabucco Zerán
Translated by Sophie Hughes

Sidewalks
Valeria Luiselli
Translated by Christina MacSweeney

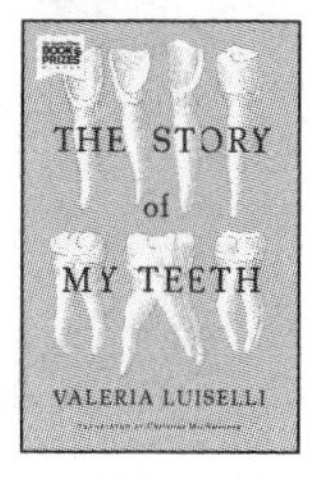

The Story of My Teeth
Valeria Luiselli
Translated by Christina MacSweeney

Empty Words was designed by
Bookmobile Design & Digital Publisher Services.
Text is set in Adobe Caslon Pro.